FALLING FOR HART

A STORY ABOUT HEARTACHE, STARTING OVER AND FALLING IN LOVE

Renee Dalton

Amazon KDP

CHAPTER ONE

FIRST, whoever says they believe in soul mates has never had their heartbroken. They never stayed in their room and cried themselves to sleep. They have obviously never walked in on their fiancé fucking their best friend from college.

These were the last three sentences that concluded my article for Pride Magazine. Those were the last three sentences my boss read out loud to me before I was fired. I loved writing for that magazine. I loved my office that overlooked the park where I would eat lunch. I loved getting emails from my readers that wanted to discuss my views or their experiences that related to the article. But that all has changed now. Everything was spiraling downward so fast, and there was nothing I could do to stop it.

They say everything happens in threes. I am just waiting for the third thing to happen... or holding my breath is more like it. I quickly realized I needed a new start to get away from this place and clear my head. The ironic thing is my new start had me going back to where it all began. The town where I grew up and realized I needed more out of life. I couldn't wait to leave New Bern, North Carolina when I was 18. During high school, I think I must have applied to every college that was at least 500 miles away from home. Moving out on my own, leaving my small town behind and trying something new was what I have wanted for a while. I remember my junior year of high school; I was at the town festival listening to all my friends talk about their summer plans. Some were working at the movies, or babysitting for their neighbors, while others were helping with their family-owned business. That was when I realized I needed to leave. I wanted more out of life than being your typical small-town stereotype waitressing at the local diner, being married by 20 and having 3 kids by 25. I knew I wanted to write and make a name for myself so when the time came, I applied to every college I could in hopes of a scholarship.

When I was accepted to Arizona University, I couldn't pack my bags fast enough. It hurt my parents a little, but deep down I knew they were proud of me. Now, here I am running back home.

I reach down for a sip of my Red Bull and try to hold my breath so I can't taste it. I hate the taste of all energy drinks, but I need something to keep me alert. All 2,200 miles of driving across the country to New Bern wouldn't be bad if I had a road trip buddy. Maybe this road trip alone will be good for me especially since I have a lot to think about now that I have no fiancé, job or home.

I try to gulp the last few sips of my energy drink down when the car jerks to the right and I nearly spill my drink everywhere. I don't know what I could have hit, but now there is a consistent thumping sound coming from under the car. I grip the steering wheel because I know what is wrong. This has to be a flat tire.

"You have to be fucking kidding me!" I guess this is number three. It was only a matter of time before the third unfortunate incident struck.

I start to pull over on the side of the interstate so I can take a look at what is in store for me. Great, not only is it a flat tire but the rim is bent. There is no way I can change this. One thing I know how to do is change a flat tire and I can thank my dad for that. He made sure when I was learning how to drive, to teach me how to change a tire, but I can't do it if the rim was bent. That I knew for sure. Now what am I supposed to do? I am still about 400 miles from home and it would cost me a fortune to have my car towed. I wipe my hands on my cut off shorts and close my trunk.

I look around and there is not a car in sight. Of course, this has to happen in the middle of nowhere. I lock up my car, grab my phone and purse and start to head toward the exit. Walking on the side of the interstate alone is not how I planned for this road trip to go. I guess it could be worse though, it could have happened at night with all the weirdos out there. Then I would really be screwed.

About 30 minutes later I finally make it off the exit and I see a small strip of stores, a gas station named Pat's and a bar named Rusty's. This town looks very run down and could use a serious facelift but what choice do I have. I take a deep breath and start to walk toward the gas station.

The bell chimes on the door as I step inside the store. It smells musty like it's been closed for weeks. All I keep thinking about is how this is the perfect beginning to every horror movie. The guy behind the counter stands up and coughs and I realize I was standing in the middle of the store looking completely out of place.

"Hey there, sweet pea. The names Pat. What can I help you with?" His smile is genuine but he's missing at least 3 teeth. I can't help but smile back.

"Hi, my tire is flat and I think the rim is bent." I must have been the only person he has seen all day. He quickly grabs his toolbox and keys and on the way to the door he flips the sign from Open to Closed.

"Well let's go get that car of yours, darling. What's your name?" He doesn't wait for me to answer. He opens the door and walks out, holding it open from the outside. As I leave, he smiles, points to his truck and locks up the store.

"Thank you, are you sure this is okay?" I hop into his pickup and the truck starts to rumble to life. "My name is Tiffany Pearce. This is really nice of you for helping me Pat."

No more than 20 minutes later we are pulling back into Pat's garage and sweat is running down my chest and forehead. I can't believe he doesn't have A/C. It's almost 100 degrees outside today.

"Alright darling, I think I should have this fixed in about 3-4 hours. There is a restaurant across the street if you get hungry while you wait."

I grin and shake Pat's hand. He is such a sweet man. He reminds me of Papa Joe back home. "Thank you so much Pat. I am starving. I'll be back in a little while."

When I step outside, I quickly realize that the restaurant Pat was talking about was indeed that old rundown looking bar, Rusty's. It's that or gas station food, I guess. I make my way across the street and as I walk up to the door, I try to dodge broken glass in the parking lot. I can only imagine what the inside of this place looks like.

I open the door and I'm immediately surprised. I wouldn't call it old. I think the word charming would be more appropriate. The bar, tables, chairs and floor are all wood. There is an old jukebox in the corner playing *Summer of 69, by Bryan Adams* and a stage that looks like it's used for karaoke. On the other side is a dartboard that looks like it has seen its fair share of games, and a pool table.

Besides a few guys sitting at the end of the bar laughing, the only other person is the bartender. As soon as the door closes, they all turn and look at me for a moment before they return to their conversations. I make my way to the bar and sit on the opposite end to avoid it being weird.

The bartender finishes serving the guys another round of beer and makes his way over to me, handing me a paper menu.

"Hey, I am Steve, what can I get for you?" I glance at the menu. "I'll have a large order of cheese and bacon fries and an Angry Orchard please."

He smiles and hands me my beer. "The fries shouldn't be too long, okay?" He takes my menu and tosses it on the back counter before walking in the back, probably to tell someone my order because he didn't write it down or enter it in the computer.

As I wait for my food, I glance around and notice how tidy the place is. Pictures are hanging on the wall of what I'm guessing is the owner with random people, maybe his regulars. I am surprised about this place. It's a nice neighborhood bar and it kind of reminds me of back home and just like that my gut-wrenching pain comes back and reminds me why I am here in the first place.

No more than 10 minutes have passed and the door to the bar opens. At first all I can see is a bright light from the outside until the door shuts. The guy walking in is at least 6 feet. He's lean but looks like he works out regularly. His hair is dark brown, cut short and he has some stubble on his face. He is gorgeous.

I quickly look away and take a swig of my beer. When I look back up, he's walking toward the empty seat next to me. My heart pounds and I get butterflies in my stomach. What the hell is wrong with me? I am supposed to hate all men right now.

"Is this seat taken?" The guy points to the chair next to me and I shake my head, moving my purse to the other side of me so he can sit down.

He smiles and sits down, holding up his finger to get the bartender's attention. "Whatever you have on tap, and another round for...." He turns to me and I realize he is waiting for me to say my name. "Tiffany...and thank you, but you don't have to order me a drink."

He smiles and holds out his hand, "I know I don't have to. My name is Darren Hart."

I start to shake his hand but quickly let go. I feel a spark and my face immediately starts to get hot. I can tell I am blushing. "Thank you for the beer, Darren."

I pick up the beer, bringing it to my lips to take a sip. This is strange. I never had a guy just come over and start talking to me like this before. I look over and watch him downing his beer. Every gulp he takes I can see his Adam's apple bobbing up and down.

I take another sip and glance over again and he is staring at me. I lick the beer off my bottom lip and it's like I am in a trans. The bartender returns with my cheese fries and I snap back to reality.

It's a huge basket of fries and there is no way I can eat all of this. "Please help yourself, I had no idea the order would be this large." They look good, or maybe I am just that hungry, either way, I don't care. I grab a few fries and eat them trying really hard to not get any food on my face.

He reaches for the fries and nods his head at me, "Thank you. What else is good here?"

I shake my head because I have no idea. The jalapeño poppers were going to be my next choice though, "No idea, I've never been here before today."

He takes another swig of his beer and orders Jalapeño poppers. Over the next 15 minutes we are laughing and making jokes. I can't believe how easy it is to talk to him. Once the poppers arrive, I grab one and start to nibble at it. I hear a small chuckle and look over. He has a smile on his face and is shaking his head back and forth.

I raise my eyebrows slightly, "What's so funny?"

He leans over close to my ear and whispers, "You are adorable sitting here drinking beer and eating bar food... and you also have cheese on the side of your lip."

My mouth drops open and he starts laughing. I am not used to someone being that forward. I smile and look down for a second feeling my face turn red from embarrassment. I can feel his eyes are still on me.

"So, are you from around here Tiffany?"

I think about how detailed I want to get. It's such an open question, but I decide to make it as brief as possible.

"Nope, far from here actually. I am driving to see my parents and I had some car trouble. It's being fixed across the street actually, so I am just buying some time."

Over the next hour, more and more people walk into the bar and we are now touching leg to leg because the bar is packed. I start to let my guard down and I am feeling more confident. It usually takes me a few beers to let loose. Something about being away, nobody knowing me or my past is appealing. I could be anyone and do anything with no judgment or people feeling sorry for me.

I lean over and touch his knee to steady myself from losing my balance, "Hey, want to play darts or pool? Both are free now."

He looks over and has the biggest grin on his face. "You are on peaches."

We stand up and grab our beers, did he just call me Peaches? He puts quarters in the side of the table and then starts to rack the balls.

I chalk up the tip of the pool stick and start to position myself to break. I pull back and hit the white ball. It hardly does anything to break apart the rest of the balls. He starts to laugh and takes a swig of his beer.

"Okay let's try that again." He stands behind me and positions his hand on mine to show me how to hold the stick. He places his chin on my shoulder whispers in my ear, "The trick Peaches is to let the stick slide between your fingers and don't keep a tight grip on the stick." He is so close to my ear, that his lips are touching my ear lobe.

"That feels good, I mean better." I quickly snap out of it and realize what I said. He starts to back away to give me room and I hear a small growl from under his breath. He clears his throat again.

I pull back and drive the stick forward. It breaks all the balls apart and a solid purple ball goes into the left corner pocket. I start to do a little dance around the table while I look for my next shot.

He smiles and tilts his beer toward me to cheers, "Nice. See all you had to do was relax your grip a little."

I lean forward and try again but miss. Now its Darren's turn. He is much better than me and continues to sink ball after ball.

"Hey, I'll go get the next round, okay?" I grab my purse off the table.

He looks up as he hits the ball, "Are you sure?"
Of course, he sinks in the next shot. I shake my head and laugh as I start to walk away. What a showoff.

I yell as I walk to the bar, "Yes, I need another round for the beating you are giving me." I can hear him laughing and I swear I can feel his eyes burning into my back as I walk up to the bar. I want to turn around to see if he is staring at me, but I don't.

There is a long line so it takes me a while to place my order. When I finally make it to the counter and start to tell the bartender what I want, some rude guy bumps me aside and screams that he wants two Jack and Cokes.

"Umm...excuse me, I was next in line." I roll my eyes and just as I am about to say my order again, the guy puts his arm around me and gives me a peck on the cheek.

"Well well well… you are not from around here are you sweetie?" What's with this place? Before I even had a chance to respond, his arm is ripped off me and the guy is pushed backward. Out of nowhere Darren is in the middle of us and the guy is still trying to figure out what happened.

"What the hell is your problem man?" The guy looks confused and scared at the same time. However, Darren looks like he is about to break the guy's neck. I have seen my fair share of bar fights from college and I know what is about to happen. I don't need more issues on this road trip.

I reach up and touch his shoulder whispering, "Hey let's get out of here and get some fresh air." Luckily for me, that's all it took to snap him back to reality.

"Are you okay though? Did he hurt you?" I can see the concern in his eyes.

"Yea I'm okay. It's getting too packed in here anyways. Let's just go." I grab my purse and we start to walk out together.

I feel his hand touch the lower part of my back as he glides me out the door of the bar. We walk down the street and end up waking through a small park. I have no idea where we are going. My heart is pounding slightly because, I have no idea what I am doing. This isn't like me.

He motions toward a small picnic table and we both sit, "So where are you from?"

I am not sure how much I want to disclose to him. Telling him too much can scare him off, and I don't want him to feel bad for me. I am tired of everyone looking at me like I am some beaten little puppy. I decide the less detail the better… For now, anyway.

"I am originally from North Carolina, but for the last 7 years I lived in Arizona. I went to college there and then worked at a Magazine for a while. What about you?" I prop myself up on top of the table.

"Oh cool, I am from North Carolina too. Well really Georgia but I moved to North Carolina about 6 months ago. I am just visiting here for work."

I smile, "Oh I love Georgia. I went to Savannah for a girl's trip last year. We had so much fun."

"Yea I use to live right outside of Savannah. My buddies and I would go there all the time."

We sit in silence for a few minutes when Darren grabs ahold of my hand and starts to draw small circles on my palm with his finger. I can't believe we both live in North Carolina. I wonder where in North Carolina he is from but I am afraid to ask.

He lifts my hand to his lips and kisses my hand. "What are you thinking?"

I let out a breath of air that I didn't realize I was holding in. I don't know why I am so nervous. Maybe now that I know we are from the same state, it freaks me out.

"I don't want to leave Darren, but I should go and check on my car. They said it should be ready by now." I start to hop down and he grabs my waist to stop me from moving.

"Can I drive you to the place at least? It's getting late and I don't want you to walk alone."

I lean back on the table and I feel his hands tighten on my waist. I touch his hand and I feel that spark again. "Why do you call me Peaches anyways?"

Darren starts laughing, "You are sweet, just like a Georgia Peach."

He bends forward and kisses me. The kiss starts soft and sweet but I can feel him start to take charge. His tongue moves aggressively with mine. It's like he is controlling my mouth like it's his to own. I have never been kissed like this before. When I was with Todd, he never made me feel this way. Honestly, with Todd half the time I was on guard when kissing him because I never knew how it was going to play out. One minute he was sweet and romantic, and the next he was cold and didn't want anything to do with me.

I can barely catch my breath and force us to break apart. I tell Darren I need to leave. I don't want to but I'm afraid if I don't do it now, I will want more and I can't do more right now. Not when I am running from one failed relationship. If I am being honest, what I want is him to kiss me and take me there on the picnic table. I want him to give me a reason to stay longer, but he doesn't.

Darren nods and helps me down. There is a part of me that's disappointed he didn't try to push me. My head and heart are telling me two different things. I am conflicted, but deep down, I know I can't have a one-night stand with someone I just met. I am not that girl and have never been that girl. I was always the goody goody, even in high school. In college all my friends would talk about the guys they hooked up with, but not me. I was the one that either stayed home or had plans with her long-term boyfriend.

Darren walks me back to his car and he takes ahold of my hand. I just spent the last few hours with a total stranger and I never felt more connected to someone in a long time. It makes me sad that we are about to say goodbye and go our separate ways.

We are both silent while he drives us across the street to Pats. I see my car ready to go sitting out front and point to my car so Darren can park next to it.

"Just a second, I need to go get my keys inside." I walk inside leaving Darren outside by his truck.

"Hi Pat, is my car all fixed up?" I smile and walk toward the counter where he is sitting.

"Sure thing darling. Now you drive safely back home to North Carolina and if you are ever back in town make sure you stop by." Pat takes my credit card and after a minute hands me my receipt and shakes my hand.

Pat was so sweet and I was lucky my car broke down where it did. It's nice knowing there are still genuinely nice men out in the world.

When I leave the store, Darren is leaning against my car waiting for me. He looks amazing. I don't understand the effect he has on me. We just met and only spent a few hours together, but I feel like I have known him forever.

"Darren, thank you for waiting with me while my car was getting fixed. This has been nice." I look down and play with my keys, not knowing what to do next. I am trying to play it cool but deep down I want him to kiss me again.

"My pleasure Peaches. I want to see you again if that's okay. Can I have your number?" Darren starts to take out his cell phone.

My hands start to sweat. I want to see him again but I can't get hurt like my fiancé hurt me 3 months ago. I am not ready.

I look up and try not to show how upset and conflicted I am.

"I'm sorry. I think it's best if we go our separate ways."

I can see the disappointment in his eyes but he doesn't push it. Darren shakes his head and tells me to drive safe, before turning around to get in his car. I stand there watching him drive off and I have to keep telling myself over and over again that what I am doing is the right thing. I start my car and as I start to pull out of the parking lot, I catch myself smiling. Of course, I am sad, because I like Darren and I didn't think I would be open to talking to another guy, let alone want to see him again after what Todd did to me. But today was the first day in 3 months that I smiled. And I have Darren Hart to thank for that.

CHAPTER TWO

I wake to my cell phone ringing. I glance at the screen and see I have 3 missed calls and they are all from my sister, Maggie.

"This better be important Mag's!" My eyes are still closed. I am exhausted because I didn't pull into a hotel until around midnight.

"Tiff, where are you? I thought you would be here for breakfast?" I rub my head and yawn as I sit up to look at the clock.

"I had some car trouble yesterday afternoon and I had to wait to get my tire fixed. I should be there around 1 p.m."

I know I have to get up and start getting ready so I force myself out of bed and head to the bathroom to pee. I still have Maggie on the phone and she is rambling about how our parents are throwing a 4th of July cookout tomorrow. I roll my eyes and make a few noises so she can tell I am still listening. The last thing I want is to be around my entire family. I am not ready to explain to everyone why Todd and I broke up.

"Look Mag's I don't want to cut you off, but I need to jump in the shower if I am going to get back on the road soon."

We say our goodbyes and I turn the shower on. In the next 6 hours I will be returning to my small-town home. Yay me! I am not ready to face my family and longtime childhood friends. After a nice hot shower and a quick coffee break, I am back on the interstate and heading East. It's a nice day so I roll my windows down and turn up the music. I can't believe I'll be back in New Bern today, starting over, and seeing everyone. It's been a while since I came back home to visit.

After running through my 90's playlist at least twice and stop for a quick smoothie I am finally in New Bern, North Carolina. I pass the sign *Welcome to New Bern* and shake my head. This place has not changed one bit. It's a small little town, with mom and pop shops. We have a few streets downtown that hold most of our stores and restaurants and it dead-ends into the town's marina. It's pretty, especially in the fall when all the trees start changing colors. I call Mag's to let her know I am almost here.

"Hey, I should be pulling up in about 2 minutes. Are you home?" I hear whispering in the background.

"Hello!" I am starting to get annoyed. What the hell is she doing?

"Yes, sorry Tiff. Amanda is here. We are making cookies for tomorrow's cookout." Great. Amanda was Maggie's best friend and she really got under my skin. But I haven't seen her in 4 years so maybe she will be different. I smile and convince myself to try and be nice. People change, right?

"Okay well I am pulling onto our street now. I'll see you in a few."

As I drive down my parent's street, I notice everything looks the same. It's like I have gone back in time. I am surprised by how comforting it feels.

I pull up to my parents' house. They still have the tire rope swing hanging in the front yard and there is still the small dent on the side of the mailbox from when I ran into it driving my dad's riding lawnmower. I am starting to think that maybe coming back home is exactly what I need. Clearly Arizona did not work out for me.

I park the car behind my dad's truck and open my trunk to get my suitcase out. I shipped the rest of my stuff that was too big to pack and it should be arriving in a few days. I start to walk up to the house and I see my parents standing on the front porch waiting for me. They are smiling and my mom is waving ecstatically. My parents are so cute together. They have been with each other since high school. I always wished I would find someone that looks at me the way my dad still looks at my mom. I have always admired their relationship. They make it look easy. They never fight, they are always together, whether its watching tv or sitting out back cooking on the grill. They enjoy each other's company, and you can tell they are best friends.

The front door opens and Maggie runs out toward me. She cracks me up because she is always so high spirited and bubbly. Maggie hugs me, "I missed you so much, you skinny bitch! It's been way too long." She spins me around and we both start laughing.

Then my parents both hug me and tell me they have my room all ready for me. Oh yea, my room. I can't believe I am moving back in with my parents and will be staying in my childhood room.

My dad grabs my bags from me and walks into the house, "Tiffany are these all your bags?".

"Yes dad, I have the rest being shipped." I follow my dad into the house where Amanda is holding open the door for everyone.

"Tiffany you look so great. Maggie has been so excited for you to come back home." I smile and half-hug Amanda as I walk inside.

"Thanks, it's good to see you too Amanda." Maggie and Amanda are both 2 years younger than me. They have always been joined at the hip. I guess I never realized how annoying that was until now. Now that I have no best friend that is. Or maybe it's just me being jealous.

I carry my bags up to my old room and see my parents remodeled the upstairs and it looks nice. I wonder when they did all this. As I unpack and hang up my clothes in the closet, Maggie and Amanda come in and hand me a glass of wine.

"Oh gosh, you guys are the best!" I need to make a run to the local store to stock up. Especially if I am staying at my parents' house. I take another swig and place the glass down.

"So, fill me in, what's new?" Amanda and Maggie glance at each other trying to figure out what they should or shouldn't say.

"Okay look let's not make this awkward. Yes, Todd cheated on me with she who shall not be named. Yes, I broke off the engagement and moved back home to start my life over." I roll my eyes and pick up my wine glass.

"Todd just turned out to be a different person then we all thought he was. I mean now that I look back on our relationship, I don't know how I never saw it before. Todd was rude to me. He would make comments about my clothes and tell me I can't pull it off, or when I would try and make dinner, there was always something wrong with it. I never feel like he appreciated me."

Amanda sits up, "You know what? Fuck Todd! He doesn't deserve you. You have a great group of friends; an amazing family and you don't need him or that backstabbing whore of a friend."

I raise my eyebrows. Maybe Amanda has changed. I think I can get on board with the new version of her.

Maggie raises her glass, "Cheers to that." *Clink.* "Okay so nothing is new here. Shocking I know! You get to meet Ryan finally. He will be here tomorrow."

Ryan was Maggie's boyfriend. They have been dating about a year now. You can hear how happy she is every time we spoke on the phone. She seems to be in love and I can tell Ryan has been good for her. She has grown up a lot over the last year. I am so proud of her.

Maggie has known Ryan for about 2 years but they didn't start dating until she got a job working for a local law firm in town. Ryan's parents own the Veterinary clinic next door, which is where Ryan works as a Vet. I guess after seeing each other every day, it's bound to happen and was only a matter of time before they started dating.

"You know, I can tell how happy you are Maggie. I am so excited you found a good guy. What about you Amanda, seeing anyone?" She smiles and starts to raise her eyebrows up and down.

"Actually, yes I met him about 2 months ago. He just moved into town. He is so sweet and Tiffany when I say he is sexy as hell, that is an understatement." Amanda starts laughing and Maggie nods.

Great. Not only will I be at a cookout with my entire family asking me what happened to Todd but now I have my sister, Ryan, Amanda and her boyfriend. Talk about the 5th wheel.

I smile and try to seem happy for them both, "That's great. I can't wait to meet everyone."

I finish unpacking and we continue to catch up over more wine. It's nice having girls to sit and talk with again. Since the incident I sort of distanced myself from everyone. I didn't realize how much I needed to just relax and hang out before tonight.

* * *

The next day I woke up to the aroma of bacon and coffee lingering in the house. One thing I did miss was my mom's cooking. I make a mental note to watch out though. My mom's cooking is amazing but the last thing I need is to gain weight. I put on my robe and threw my hair in a messy bun on top of my head. I made my way into the kitchen and as I walked in everyone becomes quiet.

"Well good morning. Do I look that bad for everyone to stop talking?" My mom stands up from her chair and gets me a cup of coffee.

"Don't be silly Tiffy, we were just discussing what we were going to tell the family if anyone asks today about Todd."

I roll my eyes. "Oh, come on. Why is it anyone's business

anyway? How hard is it to say they decided to go their separate ways?" My mom hands me coffee and kisses my cheek.

"You are so right sweetheart. No need to worry." I took a sip of my coffee. Damn that's good. I don't know how my mom does it, but her coffee always tastes the best.

"So, what time does the 4th of July party start?" I sit down at the table and grab a few pieces of bacon.

My dad clears his throat and puts the paper down on the table. "Everyone should be arriving around 2 p.m. Tiffy."

I smile, my parents haven't called me Tiffy since they dropped me off at college. I glance outside and most of the backyard was already decorated for today and had tables set up outside. They even have the canoe and paddleboards out in case anyone wanted to use them.

"Wow you all have been busy. Is there anything left to do for the cookout?" I turn around and see my dad shaking his head no.

Maggie grabs my arm and almost makes me spill my coffee. "Yes Tiffany, we need to go to the store and pick out a new outfit for today."

I yell goodbye to my parents and try to choke down the rest of my coffee while I am being dragged away, arm in arm with Maggie.

Two hours later, Maggie and I are trying on clothes in the dressing room. She has already dragged me to three different stores, all of which I haven't found anything, but this store seems hopeful. So far, I like everything I have tried on.

"Tiff, I still can't believe you drove from Arizona to North Carolina by yourself. Were you scared?"

"Why would I be scared?" I yell over the dressing room wall while I try on clothes.

"Well your car broke down right? I would have freaked out Tiffany!"

I start to laugh because it was true. There is no way she would have walked 30 minutes to find help and then go sit in a bar with a stranger for 2 hours. I started to think about Darren, wondering if he made it to North Carolina, and what he's doing. I wish I would have given him my number now. I didn't even realize it until my sister had snapped her fingers to get my attention that I was completely zoned out.

"Earth to Tiffany. What the hell were you just thinking about?" I started smiling and she knew it was juicy.

"You better tell me why you are smiling like you have the biggest secret in the world."

By the time we both find our outfit for today and pay, I tell her every steamy detail about Darren. How we met at the bar while I was waiting for my car to get fixed, played pool, and how we kissed at the park. I tell her how he wanted my number but I refused and regret it now.

"I can't believe you didn't give him your number. You are hot, available, and you need to get yourself some."

"Hey!" I slapped her butt, laughing, as we walk back to the car. It's sad but true. Part of me wishes that I gave him my number. Now I will never know if Darren Hart is the one that got away.

After we arrive home, I don't have much time before the guests start to arrive. I take a quick shower, do my makeup and change. Because it's the 4th of July, I wanted to be festive but still look cute. I picked out a cute royal blue romper. I paired it with a small gold necklace and I already had royal blue sandals with a touch of gold to tie it all together. I curled my hair a little just to give it some volume and then pinned it up in a loose ponytail with some loose strands hanging down. I kept my makeup light but added a little extra mascara and eye shadow to make my eyes pop.

I can hear the car doors starting to shut one by one which could only mean everyone is starting to arrive. I take a deep breath and prepare for what I am about to walk into. I give myself a little pep talk before heading downstairs toward the party. Just my luck as I start to make my way to the backyard my grandmother and aunt stop me.

"Oh, my dear, how are you holding up? I can't believe you guys broke off the wedding." My aunt smiles, and I give them both a hug.

"It's okay. Really. It's for the best." They both look at me like I am this sad little puppy who lost its way. I tell my grandma I will catch up with her later and I turn and walk outside to the backyard. I need a beer or four.

Two hours and I don't know how many drinks later, I start to unwind. The music was playing, people were talking, playing games and having fun. I pretty much made my rounds and said hello to everyone already. It's been nice catching up but I am exhausted telling everyone what happened and how I am living at home until I find a job.

My sister spots me and starts to wave me over. Finally! "Tiff come here. Ryan this is my sister. Tiff this is Ryan." I give Ryan and Maggie both a hug.

"It's nice to meet you Ryan. I have heard nothing but nice things about you." I sit down at their table and over the next 30 minutes we start talking about our summer plans and end up deciding to take a weekend lake trip together. Since its North Carolina, it won't start getting cool outside until late September early October.

Maggie stands and stretches. "Okay people let's play a game. Ryan you get us a few beers and that bottle of rum over there. The game is Flip, Sip, and take a shot. The object of the game is to flip a coin in the air and call it. If you get it right, everyone takes a sip except you. You pass the coin to your right for the next person. If you get it wrong only you take a sip. Flip the coin and try again. If you get it wrong again, you take a shot and pass it to your right."

Ryan brings us back each a beer along with a bottle of rum and 3 cups. "Okay ladies let the games begin."

After about 15 minutes and 3 shots I feel good. Not drunk, but good. I hear my sister starting to slur her words a little and then she yells, "Hey girl! Over here, come and join us."

I look up and see Amanda heading toward us. Amanda gives me the look and as she hugs me, "So, she's been drinking huh?"

I can't help but laugh. My sister is hilarious with a buzz. I turn around to grab my beer when I hear Amanda say, "Everyone this is Darren, Darren this is everyone."

As I turn, I nearly spit out my beer. I tried to swallow it but instead I started choking.

"Oh gosh Tiff, are you okay?" Maggie starts rubbing my back.

I nod my head yes and give my sister a look of death. I

needed to get out of here and fast. How is this happening? You got to be kidding me. Everyone is looking at me like I am crazy.

Then it happens. He speaks and I start to lose it. This has to be a bad dream.

"Hello everyone, it's nice to meet you. Thank you for inviting us." Wow his voice is even sexier than I remember it being. I need to excuse myself and clear my head.

I smile and take another sip of my beer. "Excuse me, I need to use the restroom." As I walk inside, I quickly glance back and I see Darren staring right at me. Holy hell, I am in some serious trouble.

I go to the bathroom and fix my makeup taking longer than I need to. I don't have the guts to face him or the courage to leave the bathroom. Finally, after talking myself into it, I take a deep breath and grasp the courage to leave. Maybe he left after seeing how freaked out I was. That would be the respectable thing to do in this situation.

I open the door and as I turn the corner I smack right into a wall. But it's not a wall. It's a hard chest of muscles. I look up to see Darren staring down at me smiling. "Hey Peaches."

I slowly back away shaking my head, "What are you doing here?" My lip starts to tremble. Oh God, don't cry, don't cry.

He grabs my hands and pulls me into him. I can smell his cologne, and his minty breath. "You look amazing Tiffany."

I push away and stand there staring at him, "Why are you here?"

"Look I am just as surprised and you are. When Amanda told me we were invited to a party at Maggie and Tiffany's house, it never crossed my mind it was the same Tiffany that I met 400 hundred miles away, who I had an amazing time with and wouldn't give me her number." He seems annoyed.

I take a deep breath and look behind him to make sure nobody is coming. The last thing I need is someone thinking we are together.

"Yes, I get that, but how is this happening? We met two days ago, and now you are standing in my parent's house." I am starting to tear up. Why do I have such bad luck? If I didn't have bad luck, I wouldn't have any at all.

"You have a girlfriend and yet you were making out with me the other day." I shake my head and start to walk past him. He grabs my hand and I stop to look up at him. I don't care that I have tears in my eye.

"Please wait, it's not like that. When I first sat down and we started talking it was innocent. But then I felt this connection with you and I knew I had to get to know you. Yes, Amanda and I are together, but it's not that serious. We have been on a few dates over the last 2 months, that's it."

I cannot do this right now. I don't respond to Darren. I keep walking toward the door without saying a word. I need to be alone and think about how I should handle this mess I am in. There is no way I am going to be the person to cause drama after being in town for only 2 days.

CHAPTER THREE

I can't join the rest of the group, especially Darren and Amanda right now. I walk past the kitchen, grab a half-open bottle of wine and sneak out the side door toward the lake. Even though we didn't have a boat, we still had a pier. Growing up we used to take turns jumping off the pier to see who can do the best cannonball. I sit down at the edge of the pier and dip my feet into the cool water. It's almost 9 p.m. and most of the guests have started to leave but I can still tell that Maggie, Ryan, Amanda and Darren are outside in the backyard. Mostly because I can hear Maggie laughing. I love my sister, but she can get loud when she drinks. She has one of the infectious laughs where it makes you laugh just listening to her laugh.

I start to peel off the label from the wine bottle, not paying attention that someone is walking up behind me. Ever since I was little, I would peel off the labels. I think it used to be a nervous habit of mine. It drove my family nuts.

"Are you coming back to join us?" I look up and see Darren staring down at me. When I don't answer, he starts to sit down next to me and I quickly jump up and knock my bottle of Pinot Grigio in the lake.

"Son of a bitch Darren.... Why are you even here?"

"Wait, Tiffany, please stop." He grabs my hand, but I am too quick and pull it away. Does he think we can just sit here and talk like we did the other day? He takes a few quick steps forward so he is now in front of me blocking my exit and the view of everyone.

"Please get out of my way Darren, I have nothing to say to you." I start to walk past him, and he grabs my waist pulling me up against him.

"You are driving me crazy Tiffany, please just stop and let me talk."

I throw my hands in the air, "Fine what do you want?"
He smashes his mouth to mine and I open, letting his tongue inside. I know this is wrong but right now this feels so right. He runs his hand up to my face and we slowly stop kissing. Between me feeling slightly buzzed and with how attractive he is, I knew deep down I wouldn't be able to resist him if we kept going.

Darren grabs my hand, "I am sorry about everything, I really am. I got to get back, but we need to talk about this. I can't stop thinking about you. This is crazy that I run into you here of all places and I am not letting you get away so easy this time."

I just stare at him, speechless not sure how to respond or what to do next. I stand on my tippy toes, reach forward and give him a soft peck on the cheek before walking away leaving him standing alone on the pier. It takes everything I have not to turn around and see if he is watching me leave.

The next morning, I wake up with a splitting headache. I don't normally drink that much but with the night I had, I think it called for it. I slowly make my way to the bathroom to take a shower. It's already 9 am and I can't believe my parents haven't tried to wake me up yet. I start to make my way downstairs and I realize how quiet it is. Is everyone still sleeping?

In the kitchen there is a note laying on the counter. Ahhh, my parents are at church. Maggie left with Ryan last night which means I have the house to myself for the next 2 hours. I put a pot of coffee on and head to the refrigerator to get out the creamer. My parents don't have French vanilla so half and half will have to do with some sugar. I make a mental note to go to the grocery store today to pick up a few things. I love my parents, but they are simple when it comes to things like flavored creamer or keeping wine in the house.

My mother is forever rearranging the cabinets, so I have no idea where anything is. I think it's a mix between wanting to drive my father crazy and being bored. I'm opening and closing every cabinet for a coffee mug when the doorbell rings. For a second, I decide to ignore it until I hear someone start knocking.

Not paying attention to who it is, I open the door and see Darren standing on the porch.

"You have got to be kidding me!" I slam the door closed; it doesn't take but a few seconds before he is pounding on the front door again.

"Just give me 5 minutes, please." He looks adamant and I

have a feeling he isn't going to go away this easy this time. I know I shouldn't let him in, but part of me wants to. I am fighting every urge to ignore his pleas to open the door but I fail miserably.

"Fine, make it fast." I open the door and back up to let him inside.

"I'll go as fast as you need me too, but it's not normally my style." He has this devilish grin on his face.

I roll my eyes, "Okay, I knew this was a mistake, you have to leave."

"Oh, come on, I was just joking. Look I just want to talk. I promise." Darren crosses his heart with his finger.

I roll my eyes and start to walk into the kitchen, "Would you like a cup of coffee?" I turn around and he is standing so close I can feel his breath on my face. Every breath he takes I can feel it creep up along my neck and it travels down my spine. I start to back up and run into the counter.

"I would love some coffee. Where is everyone anyway?" He put's one hand around my waist and I can feel is palm settle on my lower back.

"Maggie is staying over at Ryan's and my parents went to church." I try to not make eye contact with him. I need this to seem casual. But deep down I want him so bad. It almost feels unnatural how bad I am craving him.

He gently kisses me on my lips. I moan a little when I exhale and look down at the ground. This is bad, really bad. Darren wraps his other hand around my neck and I become putty in his arms. I lose all control and I give in to him. I am craving him more than I have ever craved anything in my life. I don't remember having this much heat with Todd ever. I don't know if it's this connection we have or the fact I have been so numb lately that I am craving attention and passion.

"God, yes." I wrap my arms around his neck. I can feel how hard he is through his pants. I start to get out of breath and break away. He moves from kissing my lips to kissing my neck and I tilt my head back to give him better access.

"You feel amazing." Darren picks me up and sets me on top of the counter. I wrap my legs around his waist. He starts to move down my neck and is about to pull my top down when I snap into the reality that I am sitting in my parent's kitchen and they can come home any minute.

"No, Darren stop. We can't do this, it's wrong. You are with Amanda." He stops kissing my neck and he leans his forehead against mine. We are both panting like we just ran a marathon.

"You are right Peaches. It's not fair to you or her. I don't know what it is. When I am around you, I lose control and can't think clearly."

"I think maybe you should leave Darren." I move my legs from around his waist and hop down off the counter. "Go home to Amanda. She is sweet and doesn't deserve this."

I walk to the front door and open it for him to leave. He walks toward me and stares at me intensely. It's earth-shattering and I don't know how I am still standing right now. On his way out the door he stops for a second, and I can tell he wants to say something but he doesn't. He doesn't say one thing. He just walks out of the house and gets in his car to leave.

I close the door and start to head back into the kitchen.

Tears are running down my face and the faster I wipe them away, the faster they start rolling down my cheeks. I still have issues of my own to resolve and the last thing I need is to get involved with someone who is in a relationship already.

I need to relax and start over. I take my cup of coffee upstairs and make myself a bubble bath. That always helps me relax and clears my head. I slowly lower myself in the tub and grab my coffee wishing it was a mimosa. I make another mental note to add champagne and orange juice to the list. I take a few sips and lean my head back, closing my eyes, trying to get Darren out of my head but it's useless though. He is all I can think about. Why did I have to meet him the other day? I need to avoid him and Amanda. I don't know how it will be possible since Amanda is always with my sister, but I can't look at her right now knowing I have this thing going on with her boyfriend. Or whatever this is with him.

* * *

A few days later Maggie and I walk into our neighborhood Wal-Mart to pick up a few things for girl's night. I have done a pretty good job avoiding Darren and Amanda. I am starting to run out of excuses, so I might have to start thinking of some other reason why I can't hang out with the group. I can tell my sister is starting to get annoyed with me. I have been either making excuses or canceling at the last minute.

"Okay Tiff, we need wine, cheese, some French bread and ice cream." Maggie starts reading off the list she made.

I look at my sister like she has lost her mind. "You had me

until ice cream. That's so disgusting Maggie."

I shake my head as I try to break apart the shopping carts. Wow, they are stuck. I start to tug on it hard. As I hold one cart with my left hand and the other cart with my right, I give it a good tug and my hand slips elbowing the person right behind me.

"Oh gosh I am so sorry." I turn around mortified and see a good-looking guy hunched over, shaking his hand at me.

"It's okay, I'll be fine. I shouldn't have been that close to you. I was reaching around you to help you break the carts free."

He straightens up and smiles. Wow! He has the bluest eyes I have ever seen. He is about 6 inches taller than me, has short dark brown hair and has a nice tan going on. Whatever he does for a living must keep him in shape.

"I appreciate you trying to help me." I start laughing and shake my head. "You know this is about right. I would be the person that goes grocery shopping and assaults someone while doing it."

He holds up his hands, "Look it was worth it. Anytime you need to take your aggression out, I am your man. In fact, just to prove to you I am fine, I would love to get your number and take you out some time."

I start to hear coughing and completely forget that Maggie is standing next to me. "Oh, I am sorry, this is my sister Maggie and I am Tiffany." We shake hands.

"Hey I am Chase. It's nice to meet you both. Look I don't mean to get assaulted and run, but I am late for work. Do you want to meet for drinks later tonight?"

It takes me a second to respond. I want to say no because I

can't get Darren out of my head, but he is with someone else. Plus, Maggie has no idea that the road trip guy and Darren are the same person. I need to try and move on. "You know what, I would love to Chase."

"Perfect. How about we meet at the Railway Pub around 7 p.m.?"

I smile and nod, "Sounds perfect, I'll see you there, Chase."

Maggie starts to push the cart into the store and I follow her. I can't help but chuckle to myself. Hopefully this will help me move on and get my mind off him.

Maggie turns to me, "So I guess girls' night is on hold then?" Oh crap. That quick I forgot. How could I be that stupid? It was the whole reason we went to the store.

"Oh, Mag's I am so sorry. I don't have to go." I put my hand on my head and my other hand on her shoulder. "Really, I don't."

Maggie starts laughing, "Don't be ridiculous Tiff. He was hot. You better go and meet him. If you don't, I will!"

"Haa, very funny. Have you forgot about, oh I don't know, Ryan?" I take hold of the cart and turn down one of the aisles.

"I am joking. But in all seriousness, you should go. It will be good for you to get out and have some fun. Besides you don't have any way to cancel now. Not showing up would be just rude!"

CHAPTER FOUR

I'm putting in my earrings when I hear a light tap on my door.

"Come on in Maggie." I turn back towards the mirror to take one last look. I must admit I don't look half bad. Pleased with how I look, I turn and face my sister as she takes a seat on my bed.

"Damn Tiffany, you look hot!" She starts to move some of the clothes I left laying out on my bed so she could sit down.

I ended up choosing a jean skirt, with black wedges, and a black sleeveless blouse. I have my hair all down and curled the ends slightly. I have always liked my hair. It's thick and dark brown. Usually in the summer the sun gives me some natural highlights. I look down at the clock and realize I have 15 minutes to get there.

"Thanks Maggie. Hey, I need to get ready and leave, wish me luck, okay?" I grab my clutch and keys and I start to leave my room, looking back to see if she is following me. "Are you and Ryan doing anything tonight since girls' night is canceled?"

"Yea we are meeting up with Amanda and Darren in about an hour. We are bar hopping down Broad St. You guys should meet up with us if it seems like it's working out."

The last thing I need is to run into Darren and Amanda. I smile, "Yea I'll see how it goes and give you a call."

The drive to the bar is quick and it only takes me 5 minutes to get there. I park my car and start to walk toward the bar when I see Chase standing outside waiting for me. He looks cute standing there with his hands in the pockets of his Docker shorts. He has on flip flops and a button-down shirt.

I smile and give a slight wave as I approach him, "Hey Chase."

He leans forward and hugs me, "Hey Tiffany. You look beautiful."

I give him a quick hug back, "Thanks, you don't look bad yourself."

We enter the Railway Pub and it has already started to pick up. We slowly weave in and out of the crowd until we make our way to the bar and order our drinks.

"So... Tiffany, are you from around here?"
I take a sip of my wine and nod, sitting it back down on the counter.

"Yea I grew up here my whole life. I moved to Arizona for college, worked there for a few years for a Magazine and recently just moved back about 2 weeks ago. What about you?"

"I am originally from South Carolina. I moved here about a year ago for work. I recently opened my own business over by the Marina. I am a boat mechanic."

Well that explains why he has such a good tan. He works on

boats all day out in the sun. "Oh, that sounds pretty cool. Do you have a boat of your own?"

"Yea I do. We should go out on it sometime." He takes a drink and raises his eyebrows to me waiting for a response.

"Yea I would love that. I know a great little restaurant on the water that serves the best crab cakes. It's this little mom and pop place but it's amazing."

He gives me a little nudge and a wide smile, "Are you saying you want to go out on another date with me?"

My face turns red immediately. I guess I was without realizing it. I turn to face him and give him a shy smile, "Yea I guess I am." I lean back slightly against the bar. I am doing my best to be flirty but not too over the top.

He leans forward so I can only hear him, "I like your shy, girl next door smile, you know that?"

Man, I need to get better at men being so forward. I give him another shy smile and take a sip of my wine. Damn it's empty.

"Here let me get us another round of drinks." He calls over the bartender and places his order. When our drinks arrive, we see a small high-top table become available. Darren points across the bar, "Hey, can you go grab that table? I will bring over our drinks."

I quickly make a mad dash for the table and sit down. We talk for another hour or so and I tell him I am looking for a local job writing for a magazine or newspaper. He asks about my family and I tell him my parents and younger sister live here in New Bern. I find out he has 1 brother who lives in Seattle and both his parents still live in South Carolina.

It's starting to get loud now that the bar is playing music and we start to lean in closer to each other so we can hear each other talk. It's nice and comfortable with Chase. Good conversation and he isn't bad to look at.

Chase leans back and puts his arm around my chair. "I guess I should have asked this earlier but are you currently seeing anyone Tiffany?"

I don't know if I should get into the long story of me and Todd. I quickly decide to dodge that bullet. "Not at the moment. I got out of a serious relationship about 4 months ago. What about you?"

He smiles and leans in toward me, "Lucky me, but no, I am not seeing anyone either. I recently got out of a serious relationship as well. Hey, you want to dance?"

We are both finished with our drinks and I am ready to start letting loose. "Yea that sounds great."

He grabs by hand and guides me out to the small dance floor. He starts to sway back and forth and grabs my arms to put them up around his neck. Then he puts his arms around my waist. We both move to *Let's get it started by Black Eyed Peas.*

I start to push my hips into him a little more and sway my head so my hair falls around my shoulders.

"I love that you can dance Chase."

"And you look sexy when you dance." He barely grazes my ear but enough to feel a tingle run down my spine. I'm really enjoying myself and for a second, I realize that I haven't thought about Darren all night. This could be the start of something.

When the song is over, I am panting hard. A mixture of exhaustion and heat and I need some air.

"Hey, do you mind if we step outside? It's getting really hot in here." I am waving my hand to fan some air toward my face.

"Yea of course, let's get out of here." We step outside and the night air has cooled down. It's comfortable and has a good breeze blowing.

"Oh, this feels so good." I grab my hair and lift it off my neck for a moment to help me cool down. I look over and I see Chase staring at me. He has this sexy grin on his face. We stand outside and talk for a bit. He asks about my summer plans and I ask what he likes to do in his free time. It's so easy to talk to him.

After a while Chase grabs my hand and starts leading us down the street. "I'm having a great time with you. Thank you for coming out tonight." Chase looks down at me as we walk holding hands.

I smile and lean my head on his arm, "I am too. I am glad I assaulted you earlier today." We both start laughing. Everything is going great tonight and I think I can see myself hanging out more with Chase.

We walk a few streets over and we end up at New Bern's local craft beer and wine bar.

"Shall we?" Chase holds open the door and I walk inside.

"Wow, good looks and a gentleman. Thank you." I start laughing and he follows me in. "I have always wanted to try this place".

We make our way to the bar and he orders a craft beer and I order a glass of Pinot Grigio, one of my favorite types of wine. While waiting for our drinks Chase gives me a small kiss on the cheek. I turn to face him, and right as I'm about to open my mouth and ask him what he's doing tomorrow, I hear a bunch of people calling my name.

"Tiff.... Tiffany, over here." I look over Chase's shoulder and my heart sinks. It is Maggie, Ryan, Amanda, and Darren. This isn't happening.

I can barely spit out the words "Oh, no" before Chase asks me if I know them.

"Yep the brown hair girl is my sister, the blonde is my friend Amanda from high school. I leave out the part that I have been secretly messing around with Amanda's boyfriend.

Chase grabs our drinks from the bar, "I am good if you want us to go over and hang out."

"Really? We don't have to. This is our date." I am praying he says, good point, and we stay put but I have a huge feeling that's not going to happen. This is going to be awkward if we go over there. I am about to tell him how I rather it be just the two of us, but Maggie and Amanda walk up.

"Hey Tiffany, who is your friend?" Amanda has the biggest grin on her face.

"Hi Amanda, this is Chase, Chase this is Amanda, and my sister Maggie."

"Hey, it's nice to meet you both." He reaches out and shakes both of their hands.

Maggie takes both drinks from Chase, "Here let me help you, come on over we have plenty of space at our table."

Chase looks at me and shrugs. We start to follow Amanda and Maggie back to the table where everyone is sitting. Oh, Lord. My night was going so well. I get to the table and start introducing

Chase to Ryan and Darren. Ryan nods and says hello but Darren just stares at Chase like he has two heads.

We sit down and everyone starts to resume their conversation. Ryan turns to me, "So Tiff, we were just talking about taking that weekend trip up to the lake if you are still interested."

I down my entire glass of wine and put on the fakest grin of my life. "Yea that sounds great, just let me know when."

Darren gets up and walks to the bar without a word to anyone. I look over to Amanda and she seems oblivious that anything is wrong. I look around at our group and nobody seems to be weirded out by this except for me.

A few minutes later Chase and Ryan are talking sports and we girls are talking about laying out at my parent's pool over the weekend. I keep up with the conversation but glance every few seconds at the bar to watch Darren.

Darren finally returns with shots for everyone, "Okay, let's get the night started." We all take the shot of tequila and throw it back. Holy crap it starts to burn my throat. I am out of wine so I grab Chase's beer and take a sip.

He smiles at me, "You know if you weren't so damn cute, I'd say hands off my beer... You okay?"

"I am now." I smile and lean forward to kiss him on the cheek. I can tell the group is staring at us, specifically Darren so I push it even further. I put my left hand up around his face and kiss his lips. He is completely on board because he doesn't stop me. Instead he continues the kiss for a few seconds. Finally, when we stop, I notice everyone is still staring at us.

"I am sorry guys." Everyone starts laughing. Maggie stands

up and starts dancing. "I love this song, come on girls let go." Amanda quickly follows her but Maggie has to grab me and guide me to the floor. Within a minute we are all dancing to *Apple Bottom Jeans by Flo Rida.*

We start dancing together and I look over. I can see all the guys staring at us. Amanda starts yelling over the music, "Oh my God Tiffany. He is so hot! Where did you find him?"

I turn to her and start laughing, "We met at the grocery store earlier today and he asked me out." We continue to dance and grind up against each other. I feel someone behind me and they wrap their hands around my waist.

"Hey beautiful." I can tell its Chase, and my heart starts pounding. I don't know if it's from him touching me or if it's because I know Darren is watching us.

I turn around and wrap my hands around his neck. We start dancing and out of the corner of my eye I look over at our table and I can see Darren staring at me. He looks kind of pissed, not sure why though. He is with Amanda. He needs to see that this is wrong and what he's doing isn't fair to her.

After the song has stopped, we head back to the table and Chase orders us another round while I leave to go to the bathroom. I can see my hair in the mirror and it's a mess from dancing. I try to comb in with my fingers when the bathroom door opens.

"Darren what the hell are you doing in here?" I throw my hands up and start to walk toward him but he quickly shuts it. "What the hell Darren?"

"What the hell? What the hell are you doing with that tool bag, Tiffany?" He looks furious and it makes me happy that he is jealous.

"Not that it's any of your business, but he is my date tonight." I try to grab the handle to open the door and Darren grabs my wrists and holds them down to my side.

He is extremely close to me and starts to move my hair from my neck with his nose and lightly kisses my ear.

"You are making me jealous on purpose Peaches." He lightly kisses my neck and then brushes the hair out of my eyes. "I am serious when I say I want to see what this is between us. We owe it to each other to figure it out."

Darren starts to kiss down my neck again and licks my collar bone. Holy crap I want him so bad. I start to moan in frustration because I want more. I want him and not for a few minutes secretly in the bathroom of a bar, I want him in my bed and all to myself.

Darren stops, "As much as I want to continue this, we need to get back. They are probably wondering where we are."

He adjusts himself and takes a few deep breaths, leaving the women's bathroom. Why does he always do that? He gets me all hot and heavy and then walks away. He is toying with me and I can't take it anymore. I need to stop falling into whatever this is. I adjust my clothes and fix my hair before returning to our table feeling both guilty and annoyed.

"Hey Tiffany, we were going to head out in a few mins." Maggie gives me an exhausted look.

Thank God. I am exhausted too, "Yea that's fine. I was going to see if you were ready to leave Chase?"

"Yea I am ready when you are." He stands to say goodbye to everyone and we all walk outside to leave.

Chase grabs hold of my hand and we walk slowly back to our cars, "I had a really good time tonight Chase. Thank you for taking me out."

I lean against my car and take out my phone. "Sorry my friends' kind of hijacked our date. I didn't expect them to be here."

I hand Chase my cell phone. "Here put your number in my cell." Chase takes my phone and enters in his number and hands it back to me. I call his cell and he removes it from his pocket, "There now you have my number too."

Chase leans forward and kisses me on the corner of my mouth, "Have a good night beautiful, sweet dream."

It was a nice kiss and perfect for the first date but something feels off. Weird almost. Like its being forced. I get into my car and start to back out while Chase stands off to the side. He waves goodbye and watches me drive away before he turns and walks to his car. I keep looking in my rear-view mirror as I drive away and I am sad. Chase is a great guy. He is attractive, sweet, polite and successful... but he is not Darren.

CHAPTER FIVE

It's been one week since Chase and I went out on our date. We texted a little back and forth but we haven't made plans to meet up again. I don't know if he can feel it too, or if we have both been really busy but the conversations have been more of a filler then two people trying to get to know each other.

I was able to secure a job working as a journalist for a local newspaper in town and the best thing is, I can work from home. It wasn't anything extravagant but it paid the bills and the hours were flexible. Now that I found a job, it was time to find a place to move into and out of my parents' house. I was meeting Maggie for lunch today and then she was going to help me look for an apartment. I walked into a local café in town and spotted Maggie sitting down looking at the menu. It's good to be back home. I miss seeing my sister and having lunch with her. Yeah, it had to take a horrible thing for it to push me back this way, but now I am thinking it's for the best.

"Hey Maggie, what looks good?" I sit down and start to pick up the menu and read it. She doesn't respond so I look up at her to see what's wrong.

"I need to ask you something, and just remember I am your sister and I love you."

"Okay, this sounds serious, you have my attention." I am worried. Maggie is normally so carefree and not serious at all.

"Amanda told me she thinks Darren is seeing someone else. I didn't say anything to you, but the night of the cookout I saw you storm out of the side of the house and walk to the pier. Then Darren came out of the house and started following you."

"Oh." That's all that I said to my sister. She just looked at me with a concerned expression. I didn't know what to say.

"Then at the bar, you both went to the bathroom at the same time. Please tell me this is a coincidence Tiffany?"

"Maggie, please...." I continue looking down at my menu to avoid eye contact. Do I come clean or lie? I usually can think quickly on my feet, but I never lie to my sister. Plus, even when I try, she calls me on my shit.

"Really that's all you have to say. I mean come on Tiff. Please tell me you guys are not messing around with each other." She sets her drink down on the table a little harder than she needed to and it made me flinch.

I look over my shoulder to make sure nobody can hear us. "Okay Maggie, look I know how it looks. But hear me out. You know the guy I met on the road when my car broke down? Do you remember what his name was?"

I can see the light bulb turns on. Suddenly Maggie looked

46

like she has seen a ghost. "Wait a minute. Are you telling me that your Darren and Amanda's Darren are the same person?"

I hate seeing my sister upset but I couldn't lie. I am horrible at it. I feel like such a bitch for putting her in this awkward situation because now her sister and her best friend share the same love interest.

"Yes, Darren is the guy I met in the bar. Mags we really hit it off. I honestly had no idea he was involved with anyone. When he showed up at mom and dad's I lost my shit. That was why I started coughing on my drink when he introduced himself." I feel so guilty and confused. How did I let myself get into this drama?

"Holy shit Tiffany. What are you going to do?" My sister looks worried.

I honestly have no idea how to deal with this situation. I mean I have two guys that are interested in me, and I like both. Darren is unavailable but we have an amazing connection together, plus I am so attracted to him. Then there is Chase. I am attracted to him too and he is great but I can't stop thinking about Darren when I am with him.

"I don't know. I told Darren we can't see each other but somehow, we keep running into each other. Why does Amanda think Darren is seeing someone else anyway?"

"She said he is acting distant and he turned her down for sex the night we all went out and ran into you and Chase. She thinks he is trying to push her away so she will break up with him."

My heart sank. I am such a horrible person and a friend. How did I get myself into this mess?

"Look Tiffany. Darren and Amanda have been dating for

almost 2 months when you guys met. They went out a handful of times but I don't think they ever talked about being exclusive. Honestly, I even remember Amanda mentioning going out with some guy about 2 weeks ago, so I don't think they are that serious. But before anything happens between you guys, Darren should either end it or come clean with Amanda."

The waitress takes our order and walks away quickly. I think she can tell we are having a heated discussion. I look at Maggie and shrug, "Just tell me what I should do?"

Maggie's phone starts to go off, and after she looks at it, she turns it around to show me that she received a text message from Amanda.

"Amanda says that she wants all of us to go away this weekend to the Lakehouse. She thinks getting away and being alone with Darren might help." Talk about bad timing.

"Oh, I don't know if that is a good idea Mag's. Every time I am near Darren there is this energy between us. I know it sounds crazy but I never felt like this before. Even when I was with Todd."

My relationship with Todd started amazing. We met in college and from the moment we started to hang out, we were inseparable. He was always the jealous type but I thought it was cute. We had issues like all couples, but once we got engaged, I could tell he started changing. He would work long hours and say it was to save up for the honeymoon, but he seemed distant and when we went out, it was like I wasn't there. He flirted with other women and when I would confront him, he would raise his voice and turn it around so I looked like a jealous control freak. But we loved each other and I just assumed we were in a funk. I didn't realize what was going on until one day I came home early from work sick, to find Todd and my best friend in our bed.

"Oh man, you have it bad, don't you?" Maggie looks at me with concern, "Maybe you should go. Look Amanda is my best friend, but you are my sister. Maybe this trip will help you both figure out what you want."

"Let me think about it. I will let you know, okay?" Lunch finally arrived and my chicken Caesar salad looks really good, but my appetite just wasn't there. I force myself to eat it anyway so my sister stops staring at me like I'm broken.

After lunch, Maggie tries to lift my spirits by planning out the rest of our day. We leave the café to go apartment hunting and it does the trick. I am so excited to finally get my stuff out of storage and move out and into my own place. I love my parents but it has only been a few weeks and they are starting to drive me crazy.

The first two apartments were duds. One smelled like cats and the other was beautiful but it was a studio and I wanted a bedroom and maybe a loft so I can work from home.

We pull up to the third apartment. It was right on Broad Street and it overlooked the marina and downtown. It was close to everything and I would be able to walk to most of the restaurants and shops which would be great. I had a good feeling about this one.

Maggie and I walked up to the gate and hit the buzzer.

"Hello?" A women's voice echoed on the intercom.

"Hi, this is Tiffany, we spoke on the phone about the apartment earlier."

"Ah yes, come on up Tiffany." The door clicked open and we both walked inside. We took the elevator up to the top floor and knocked on the door.

"Hello, come on in Tiffany. Please look around and let me know if you have any questions. It has 2 bathrooms, 1 bedroom, and a loft. All the appliances are new and the carpet was just replaced."

The realtor was young, probably mid 30's, beautiful brown hair and probably the biggest eyes I have ever seen. I laugh to myself as I walk in. I bet her fiancé never screwed around on her. I bet she isn't dumb enough to get herself into a stupid love triangle either.

Maggie coughs and I realize I was still standing there staring at her. "Great thank you for letting us see the apartment on short notice. I didn't want to miss out on it. It's in such a perfect area for me."

I walk around the apartment and start to get really excited. The kitchen was small but it was open to the living room. I liked that it had two bathrooms so nobody had to go to my bedroom. This place was perfect. The bedroom was a nice size and the closet was huge. What I really loved was the exterior brick in the living room and bedroom, it was beautiful. There was also a nice balcony that overlooked Broad Street. Since I was on the third floor, I can see the marina in the distance. This apartment was perfect for me and I can see myself living here, writing in the loft and drinking my coffee out on the balcony.

"How much are they asking a month?" I hope this was not out of my budget.

"They are asking for a deposit of first and last month's rent upfront. The monthly rent is $1,100." I was surprised. This was not a bad price for the location and the view.

"Okay, I will take it. When will it be available?" I was excited and I can tell Maggie was too.

"Wow Tiffany I am so jealous. This place is amazing." She was walking down the hallway from the bedroom.

"The apartment is available in 2 days. I just need you to sign the lease and provide a check for first and last month's rent and you can have the keys by Wednesday."

I finally felt like something was working out in my favor for once. This apartment was just what I was looking for. One more thing I can check off my list.

* * *

Two days flew by. My parents were shocked at how fast I found an apartment but they said they were happy. I honestly think they are happy to get their guestroom back. My mom uses it for her crafts. While I was staying in the guestroom, she was using the living room and I know that was driving my dad crazy.

"Hello, anybody home?" I hear knocking and then the door opening and the sound of bags ruffling.

"Hey Maggie, I am in the bedroom." Maggie walks in with a bunch of bags and tosses them on the bed, taking a seat trying to catch her breath.

"What is all this stuff?" I can't believe all the bags. Some are from Target and Bed Bath and Beyond.

"It's my little gift to you for your new apartment. I figured you would need some new towels, and some stuff for the kitchen."

I smile and walk over to my sister and hug her. "That was

sweet of you, thank you."

"Of course. So, have you thought any more of the Lake Trip?" She starts pulling the stuff out of the bags and doesn't look up at me. "Everyone wants to leave next Thursday and stay till Monday."

"Oh, I see what this is... You are trying to get me to say yes after you buy me all this stuff. Sneaky, Sneaky."

She smiles and throws a towel at me. "That is not true. I just think it would be good to get away and clear your head. Whatever happens I am here for you and I support you."

I take a deep breath and slowly let it out. "Fine, count me in." She starts jumping up and down.

"Okay now that's out of the way, I have wine chilling in the refrigerator. Let's get to work on putting your stuff away. The movers should be here in an hour with your furniture."

* * *

The next day I invite Maggie and Amanda over for wine and to see my new apartment all set up. I am just about moved in and I love all my new stuff. My parents bought me a new dining room set, and I ordered a new living room set.

The living room set has a grayish-blue couch and matching oversized armchair and the coffee table is a dark gray stained wooden table with storage underneath. Everything goes together. And the best thing about it is its all mine.

It's around 5 p.m. when Maggie and Amanda show up. I made my famous onion dip and Amanda brought a bunch of cheese for us try. We are having fun, drinking wine and talking about high school when Amanda's phone starts ringing.

"Oh, it's Darren, hold on a sec, let me get this." Maggie glances my way and smiles slightly. I almost forgot about this awkward triangle I am involved in and then her stupid boyfriend has to call her and bring it back to reality. I hear her telling him she is at my new apartment, and how it's really nice and right on Broad Street. Great now he knows where I live.

"Hey Tiffany, the guys are a block away having a beer and want to know if they can come over and see the place?" I freeze and don't know what to say. Shit, I look like an idiot.

My sister picks up on my freak out moment and chimes in, "Amanda I thought this was going to be just a girl's night." She looks at me and shrugs. I know she tried.

"It was but they asked if they could join. What's the issue anyway, we love hanging out with the guys?"

"Yea that's fine Amanda, go ahead and tell them to come over, and bring more wine." I gulp down my glass of wine and look at my sister. She starts shaking her head and smiles. This night is going to be interesting.

About 30 minutes later the guys knock on the door and Amanda jumps up to let them in. I am in the kitchen cutting up the cheese and laying out crackers Amanda brought over. I can hear them talking and saying how nice it is to have an apartment close to the downtown.

I take a deep breath and walk into the living room with the snacks. Ryan smiles and hugs me. He compliments me on the apartment and says how nice it is. Darren stands there with two bottles of wine and places them on the table.

"Hey Tiffany, the place looks great. Thank you for letting us come over." I smile and put down the cheese and cracker plate.

"You're welcome. Thank you for the wine, please help yourself to some cheese and crackers. If you guys don't want wine, there is beer in the fridge."

Ryan jumps over the arm of the couch and heads into the kitchen. "Sweet! Thanks, Tiff. Hey nice Kitchen. I like how open it is."

He walks out with two beers and hands one to Darren who smiles and sits down at the table.

"So, I hear we are all going to the lake next week. It's going to be awesome!" Ryan clinks bottles with Darren.

Amanda and Maggie are pouring the wine and I walk over to the stereo to play some music. I am trying to sync my Pandora to the stereo when Darren walks over.

"Hey, do you need help with that?" I smile and hand over my phone.

He begins to mess with the settings and sure enough the music starts playing through the speakers.

"Thanks. I would have been here all night trying to figure it out." He hands me back my phone and starts to walk away. I look at the screen and see that he wrote a message on my phone.

Can we please meet up and talk? I can't stop thinking about you.

Who does he think he is? I am trying to move on and get

passed this but he is making it difficult. I guess I'm staring at my phone longer then I think because my sister clears her throat and when I look up everyone is sitting at the table staring at me. When I start to walk over everyone starts laughing.

"Wow Tiffany, who is the guy? Oh, is it that hunky guy from last week?" Amanda starts laughing.

I decide to play along and make Darren uncomfortable. I shouldn't be the only one. "Oh no, it's this guy that wants me really bad. I met him a few weeks ago and he keeps trying to get with me. He is unavailable though." I try to keep a straight face and not laugh. Two can play at this game. Game on Darren!

Darren starts coughing and I look over at him. "You okay over there?"

Everyone turns to look at Darren and he gives me the look of death. Okay maybe this will be fun.

Amanda starts laughing... "Wow what are you going to do?"

"I'm not sure yet. Right now, I just want to have fun and date." I try to be as casual as I can, but I don't typically do casual so I don't know if they bought it.

The rest of the night I do my best to keep my distance from Darren and don't allow us to be alone together. Around midnight everyone starts to leave and I clean up the kitchen and throw away the uneaten food. I take a quick shower and start to get ready for bed but of course I am still wide away and can't get Darren out of my head. I decide to pour myself a glass of wine to help relax and when I start to walk back to my bedroom, I hear a tapping on my front door.

I look through the peephole and see that it is Darren. My

heart starts racing and I take a deep breath before opening the door.

"Hey is everything okay?" God, he looks good standing there.

"Did you get my message? Can I come in so we can talk?" I pause for a second and step back to open the door. I know I am going to regret this.

"You know you shouldn't open the door dressed like that! You barely have anything on. What if I was just a random guy?"

Crap I completely forgot I only have on a tank top with no bra and a pair of short cotton shorts. "I wasn't thinking and definitely didn't think I would have any more visitors at 1 a.m."

"Just be careful. I can't stop thinking about you Tiffany, that's why I came back tonight. I want us to get to know each other better and see what this is. Amanda and I are not exclusive." He genuinely looks sincere.

"Look I wish the situation was different but it's not. You are dating one of my friends. I can't be that girl. It's not right. Don't make this harder than it already is." I realize I am holding my wine so I take a sip and look at Darren. He is staring at me and I can feel it go right through me causing me to shiver.

"If you don't feel the same way I will leave and I will not bring it up again. But you need to be honest with yourself and me. Can you honestly say you don't have feelings for me? That you don't think about what it would be like together because I do and I know it would be amazing."

I didn't realize he started walking toward me during his rant. When he stops talking, he lifts my chin so I am looking at him, "Can you honestly say you don't wonder what it would be like if we were together? Holding each other at night, kissing each other."

"Of course, I do. This is why it's so hard. Do you think it's easy for me to see you with Amanda?" I sway my arms in frustration, forgetting I am holding a glass of wine. Wine spills out of my cup and splashes on the floor.

Darren starts to smile. He takes my wine and places it on the table. His hands start to move around my waist and he pulls me closer toward him.

"I miss you Peaches. I am a nice guy and what we have is special. When I met you a few weeks ago I was drawn to you. I know it sounds crazy." He leans in and kisses me.

I wrap my arms around his neck and we both start walking back towards the couch. Darren guides me down on the couch and I lay back to get more comfortable. I need him so much and I honestly don't think anything could make me stop right now. After a few minutes he re-positions himself and leans back against the pillows. I put one leg over each side so I am now straddling him.

I can feel his hand rubbing my back and holding onto my waist as we kiss. He starts to kiss my neck and pushes my hair to the side. "You feel so good."

I moan and that's all the response he needs to lift my tank top. My breasts are now fully exposed and he starts to kiss them. I lean back and start grinding into him. I have one hand on the back of his neck while the other is holding onto his shirt.

"Darren, please don't stop. I need you." He kisses me again and I can't think about anything else but this moment right now. I know what we are doing is wrong but right now I don't care. He stands up and I wrap my legs around his waist holding on. We kiss as he walks down the hallway to my bedroom and shuts the door. I know I should stop it but I can't fight it anymore and honestly, I don't know if I have the strength to.

CHAPTER SIX

The next morning when I wake up, I have the biggest smile on my face. I still can't believe Darren and I was together last night. It was amazing. He made me feel things I never felt before. The sex was hot and Darren knows exactly what he's doing. Just thinking about last night is making me all hot again so I force myself to get up and take a shower. I already completed my article I had to turn in for work so I decide to take the day off and treat myself.

I dial Maggie's number to see what she was doing and to invite her out to get our nails done and maybe do some shopping. I miss being able to hang out with her like this. Moving to Arizona for school was just my excuse to move away, but once school was done and I didn't move back home, I think my sister took it hard. We sort of stopped talking for a while, so now that we are getting back to doing sisterly things, it means a lot to me.

Maggie agrees to meet up but won't be available for a little over an hour or so. That's perfect and gives me enough time to get dressed and do my hair and makeup before meeting her.

After we get our nails done, we start to walk down the street and I ask to stop into a lingerie store. Nothing makes you feel sexy like new bras and underwear.

"So, have you heard back from Chase after you guys went out?" I can tell Maggie is trying to make small talk, so I go along with it.

"Yea actually he called me up a few days ago and said that he is going to try and work things out with his ex and he is sorry if he led me on." To be honest I was relieved. I didn't want to be the one to call it quits so it worked out for the best.

"Oh, that sucks, I am sorry Tiff." I shrug because it really is no big deal to me and honestly my heart wasn't in it.

"It's okay. He was nice but I don't think we had the spark, you know?" I hold up a bra and panty set. "Hey, do you like this?"

"Yea that's sexy as hell. What's all this for anyway? Did you meet someone?" Maggie's phone starts ringing. I can hear her trying to calm the person down on the other line. After a few minutes Maggie mouths to me OH MY GOSH and then I hear her tell the person on the phone to meet us for lunch. The person must have accepted the invite because when Maggie hangs up, she says that Amanda is meeting us in 30 minutes for lunch.

"Amanda, why?"

"She was hysterical Tiffany. Amanda said after she and Darren left your apartment last night, he said he was going home. She was crying so it was hard to understand her but something about wanting to surprise him. She showed up at his place and he wasn't home. She tried calling him but he didn't answer."

"Oh." I go back to looking at more sets and end of grabbing three more on the rack before looking back at Maggie.

"Wait, Tiffany you don't know anything about this do you?" I look at her and shake my head no. "Oh my God Tiffany, you didn't!"

"Maggie, do you honestly want to know because you know you can't say anything to Amanda." I give her the death stare.

"Tiffany please tell me Darren did not stay over?" She stops me as we are walking up to the register to pay.

"Look, yes okay, he came back last night, we started talking and one thing lead to another and we had sex." I walk toward the exit and push open the door. I don't even wait to see if she is following me before I start walking to the car to put my bags in.

"Tiffany this can't end well, you know that right?" Maggie looks upset and I feel like I made a huge mistake for telling her now.

"Look. I didn't mean for it to happen, it just did. But this isn't like a fling. I cannot explain it Mag's. I never felt this way about someone before and I think it is the same for him too. He said he is going to break it off with Amanda today."

"I just want you to be careful that's all. We are not in high school anymore, you know?" She hugs me and tells me she hopes I am happy and everything works out.

We walk across the street and get a table. Soon as the waiter seats us, we see Amanda walk in and she looks like she has been up all night crying.

As she walks toward us, I whisper to Maggie, "I am such a horrible person. What is wrong with me?"

Amanda sits down and orders a glass of wine. She immediately starts tearing up again. "He wouldn't answer his phone. I wanted to surprise him. I showed up to his apartment wearing a dress with nothing underneath. When he didn't answer the door, I called and it kept going to his voice mail."

Maggie hugged her and then looked at me with a guilty expression on her face. "What time was this? It had to be late."

"Around 1 a.m. It was right after we all left Tiffany's." Amanda took a huge gulp of wine and when the waiter came back to the table, she immediately ordered another.

"So, I got really upset and went to the sports bar down the street to see if he was there but he wasn't. I ordered another drink and started talking to the bartender as he was closing down." She takes another drink and looks like she is afraid to say what she is about to say.

I feel like I need to say something, but what do I say to the person who is distraught and I am the reason?

"Amanda look I am sorry with what you are going through." I reach across the table and pat her hand. I feel like a fraud.

Amanda starts to cry even harder now, and it's starting to get everyone's attention around us. I look around and can see people glancing at our table. Amanda quickly gets my attention back to her when she blurts out that she slept with someone else last night.

If on cue, Maggie and I both yell at the same time. "WHAT?"

Amanda starts crying, "I was drunk, I was pissed he was ignoring me. The bartender was cute and he was listening to me vent. He walked me back to my car but I couldn't drive home so he said he would give me a ride."

"So, what does this mean for you and Darren now? Are you going to tell him?"

Amanda wipes her eyes with her napkin and takes a deep breath, "We had sex in his car before he dropped me home. I don't even know his name. I feel like a horrible person. How could I have let that happen?"

"Sounds like you were just upset and you made a bad decision. Nobody is perfect Amanda. Maybe Darren will understand and you guys can work through this."

Amanda perks up, "Maybe. I mean we never had the exclusive talk. Maybe he won't think it's a big deal. What do you think Tiffany?"

"Me? Um, well I guess reverse the situation. Would you be mad at Darren if he slept with someone else?" Maggie gives me a nasty stare. She knew what I was doing.

"Honestly, I probably would be yes, but now that I slept with someone, I want to say I wouldn't be mad. I guess I can't answer that question."

Damn. That wasn't the answer I was hoping for. "Well I guess you need to ask yourself. What are you more upset with? The fact that you slept with someone else and you are afraid Darren will be mad? Or the fact that Darren didn't answer your calls?"

Amanda started nodding, "I guess I am more upset that he didn't answer my calls and I think he was seeing someone behind my back. Don't get me wrong, I know what I did was wrong. But it also felt right. I can't explain it. I guess that is also why I am upset. Because I am afraid of what that means. I want Darren but I don't want to settle down either."

Maggie looked confused, "What do you mean?" Yea I was lost too. Is she saying what I think she is saying?

"I guess what I'm saying is that I kind of liked that feeling of being with someone new. Darren is great but he has been distant for a while now and it shouldn't be that way. Not when we have been dating for a little over 2 months."

"Amanda, I think you know what you need to do then." Maggie gives her a sympathetic nod.

"I don't know if I can though. I don't want to be that person, you know?"

"I understand, but you need to be honest. If you don't feel that way about him anymore you can't waste any more of each other's time. That is not fair to either of you." Amanda smiles and hugs Maggie.

"Thank you for being honest with me and telling me what I should do and not what I only wanted to hear." We finish our meals and I try my hardest to dodge any more talk regarding Darren.

Later that afternoon I was sitting out on the balcony of my apartment listening to music and writing myself a list of stuff I need to pack for the lake trip in a few days. I had emptied my glass of wine so I get up to get a refill when my phone chimes. It was from Darren.

Downstairs....Can I come up? We need to talk....

I hit the buzzer and then go to unlock and open the door for Darren. He was just coming off the elevator when I opened the door. He stops in his tracks and looks at me.

"Are you okay?" I don't know what else to say to him. Is he upset? Did Amanda tell him already? Does he regret us being together last night? I have all these unanswered questions circling in my head.

He starts to walk toward me and I move back into the apartment to let him inside. "Yea I am okay. Amanda called me a few hours ago and broke up with me. She got drunk and slept with someone last night."

Wow, I can't believe Amanda told him the truth and broke it off. I know I always had an issue with Amanda but the girls got some balls for sure. I got to give it to her. I didn't think she would actually go through with it after we had lunch.

"How does that make you feel?" I don't know what else to say now and I am honestly a little shocked.

"Honestly, I feel a little guilty that she came clean and told me and I didn't tell her about us. I know that would make things hard for you, so I am not going to. I wanted to make sure you knew that, but as for Amanda and me, we are no longer together."

I sit down on the couch and he follows. I don't know what to say so I stay quiet. I can tell deep down he is upset and hurt whether he wants to admit it or not. I want to hug him and be there for him, but I also know that I am part of the problem. I don't know what he needs or wants from me. I feel so helpless.

"So, what happens next?" I am trying to mask this hopeful feeling but still seem empathetic at the same time, however I am failing horribly.

"I don't know. We both have the same group of friends so

we are going to see each other all the time. It will be weird for a little while I am sure."

It's killing me that he is upset and all I keep thinking about is us.

"What about what happened to us last night? Do you regret sleeping with me?" There is a part of me that has been so scared to ask this, but I must know. I have been trying to keep my distance from him since the 4th of July party, and he hasn't made it easy. Now I feel like I am the one hunting him and I don't like it. How did we flip flop like this?

Darren moves closer to me on the couch and grabs my hand. "Are you kidding me? You are the only reason why I am keeping my cool right now. I do not regret being with you at all. I just don't know how we can continue being together right now after everything that just happened. If we start dating it will look bad to everyone and I don't want to cause any issues for you."

I nod, "I understand and I appreciate that. Maybe we should keep our cool for a little while and see how it plays out. Are you still planning on going to the lake house on Thursday?" I raise my eyebrows and deep down I hope he says yes.

"Yea I think I still might go, but it will be kind of awkward." I shrug and lay my head on his shoulder while we sit in silence for the next few minutes.

I can feel him take a deep breath, "Maybe we should continue just being friends for right now Peaches."

A small tear leaves my eye. I blink to try and stop more from coming. I had a feeling he was going to say that. "Okay, I can be your friend."

Darren stands up, takes a deep breath and walks to the door. Before opening it, he turns and we lock eyes. My heart aches and I try to hold back tears which makes it hard to breathe. I can feel my bottom lip start to tremble. How could I have opened my heart and been so stupid? Again, here I am in the same position I was 6 months ago, getting hurt by a guy I care about. I opened my heart up to Darren and it backfired on me, leaving me alone and regretting my decision of last night.

CHAPTER SEVEN

It's been a few days since the whole Darren and Amanda catastrophe. I tried to back out of the lake trip. I really did. It would be too weird going. Especially since Darren and Amanda will be there. I couldn't imagine going on a vacation with my ex after we broke up. Especially if I slept with someone else. However, Maggie did say they all sat down and talked. They agreed to stay friends and be civil to each other. I don't know how that can work. But I give them credit for trying.

I am staring at my closet not sure what to pack when I hear my sister letting herself into my apartment.

"Tiff, are you ready? Everyone is meeting downstairs in 20 minutes." Maggie walks into my room and looks panicked. I have clothes thrown everywhere. My suitcase is empty, and I look a mess. If now was ever the time to run and hide from my sister, now would be it.

"Why are you not packed yet?" Maggie is annoyed. I can see

it in her face.

"I really don't want to go Maggie. I told you already. It's going to be too weird. I don't know if I can do this." I try not to look her in the eyes because I know she will see right through me and I will start crying.

She sits down on my bed and starts folding and putting the clothes I have thrown around in my suitcase. "Yes, you are going, and you are going to have fun. Just because Darren said he wants to be friends with you, doesn't mean it will last forever. Give him time. He is confused."

Damn. I know she would figure out the real reason. Who am I kidding? It's not because Darren and Amanda broke up. It's because Darren wants to cool it with me. I feel stupid and embarrassed. Why did I have to sleep with him?

"I know, I'm sorry. It's just I am kind of pissed. We sleep together when he is with Amanda, and then now they are broken up he wants to be just friends." I shake my head and walk into my bathroom to get my bathroom bag. "You know you are right...I didn't mean for any of this to happen. Maybe we are not meant to be. I mean we met on the road and he didn't tell me he had a girlfriend. Then we finally sleep together, and he tells me he just wants to be friends. I guess that's my sign. It's just not supposed to work out with us."

I finish packing, lock up and we start to head downstairs to meet everyone else. We are only a few minutes late. I commend myself for getting ready so fast. Soon as we walk outside, I see Amanda, Darren, and Ryan laughing.

Ryan is lifting all the bags into the back of the SUV and he's giving Amanda a hard time, "I can't believe you brought two suitcases Amanda. You do realize we are only staying for four days don't you?"

"Yes, I know that, but a girl needs her stuff. Plus, we will be in the woods away from everything. I like to be prepared." She starts laughing and gives Ryan a nudge.

"Prepared for what exactly Amanda? Do you think we are going to get stranded out there or something? This isn't Gilligan's Island." Darren starts to shake his head and hands Amanda's last bag to Ryan. Everyone is cracking up.

I walk over to Ryan and hand my suitcase to him. He gives me a sympathetic smile and asks if I am okay. Hmm, am I okay? Well let's see, No, your ass hat of a friend.... I stop. I can't keep doing this. I quickly respond that I am okay, and I appreciate him checking up on me.

Ryan smiles and closes the trunk, "Okay everyone there are three rows. I am driving and Maggie has shotgun."

We all look at each other and I really start to wish I was anywhere else but here right now. I finally speak up since nobody else does. "I'll take the last row." I start to climb in, and I can feel Darren's hand on my leg as I climb over the seat.

"I can sit back there and keep you company, Tiffany." I turn around to face him just as he enters.

"No, you can sit in the middle row with Amanda." I stare at him looking pissed off so he will get the hint that I need some space and he starts mouthing the words **Please, I want to sit next to you.**

Amanda speaks up, "Okay cool, we can play cards Darren." She starts to push him forward so she can get inside. She is oblivious to what is going on, and I am thankful. The last thing we need are questions to be asked while stuck in a vehicle with nowhere to run to for hiding.

* * *

It feels like we have been driving for forever and I can't take it anymore. Darren keeps texting me that he wishes he was sitting next to me and he wants to make this friendship work. I don't respond to any of his texts. How can he think I would be okay with just being friends after we slept together? I need to take a breather and get some air.

"Ryan can we please pull over when you see the next gas station? I need to use the restroom and get a snack."

"Yea that's fine, I need to gas up anyway." He looks in his rear-view mirror and winks at me. I give him a thankful smile and he starts to pull off the freeway onto the exit ramp. Soon as we park everyone gets out to stretch their legs and I do my best to stay clear of Darren. The last road trip I was on that involved Darren was how we got into this mess in the first place.

"Hey, does anyone want anything while I am in there?" I try to act cool, so nobody catches on that I needed to get away for a few minutes. Amanda asks for bottle water, Ryan and Maggie ask for a fountain diet coke to share and a bag of Doritos.

I start to walk toward the gas station and Darren starts running up behind me, "Hey wait up, I'll help you."

I make it inside before he catches up and I immediately go toward the wine and champagne. I pick up a bottle of champagne from the cold section and start working on getting the rest of everyone else's stuff. Champagne sounds great right about now. So, what if I have nothing to toast to. I have always had a thing for champagne. My friends used to laugh at me and ask how I can drink it, but I love it. I think it's refreshing and not as heavy as beer.

"Hey, Tiffany, why didn't you wait for me? Are you seriously mad at me because I think we should just be friends?"

I can't believe he just said that to me. He has a lot of nerve. "Are you serious right now? You come to my apartment, tell me you want to be with me, we sleep together, and then two days later you change your mind and tell me you want to just be friends. It's clear to me now you only wanted to get in my pants. You never had feelings for me. Just do me a favor and leave me the hell alone Darren!"

He stands there looking shocked and doesn't say anything. Good maybe that will shut him up for a while.

I walk to the counter to pay and leave him standing there in the middle of the store. The cashier hands me my stuff and I walk out and don't look back. I can care less if I hurt his feelings. Okay maybe I care. I feel really bad that I just yelled at him in the middle of the store. I don't know what is with me and worrying about hurting others when they hurt me first. I made a mental note to work on that.

I give everyone their stuff and Amanda asks where Darren is.

"Who knows Amanda." She looks at me confused for snapping at her.

I know I need to quickly change the subject. As I start to

climb over the seat into the back row, I tell everyone that I got us some champagne to share for the rest of the trip. Darren finally makes his way back to the SUV and climbs inside not saying a word to anyone.

"Alright let's hit the road, we have 2 more hours to go." Ryan starts to pull back onto the highway and I pop open the bottle of champagne.

I take a swig. "Here is to 4 days of not caring about anything." I hand the bottle to Amanda.

Amanda takes a drink, "Here is to friendship." She smiles at Darren and passes him the bottle.

He takes a few sips of the champagne, "Cheers to getting wasted while on this trip." He hands it to Maggie.

"Here's to making new memories." She takes a quick drink and then Ryan asks her to take another drink for him since he is driving, "Here is to skinny dipping in the lake." Maggie starts laughing and she takes another drink. "I will definitely drink to that."

The rest of the trip is uneventful. I fall in and out of sleep, while listening to Maggie sing along to the radio, and trying to ignore Amanda's constant need for attention. She had to of asked Darren 100 questions, trying to keep the conversation between them.

Two hours later we pull up to the lake house and everyone quickly jumps out and starts to unload the SUV. The house is beautiful and has an open floor plan. Most of the windows in the house overlook the entire lake. There is a fire pit in the yard and a pier that leads out to the lake with canoes. The house is rustic and charming at the same time. I think spending the next 4 days here is just what I need to clear my head and maybe I might even do some writing of my own.

Ryan starts to walk around the house opening the windows, "Okay there are enough bedrooms for everyone. Let's unpack and then figure out what everyone wants to do next."

Everyone starts to go towards the bedrooms. Ryan and Maggie share a room, Amanda picks the room at the end of the hall so that leaves the 2 bedrooms across the hall that are connected with a Jack and Jill bathroom. I'll need to see if there is a lock on the door. There must be. The first thing I do is start to unpack and open the blinds to my room so I can take in the view. It's beautiful and overlooks the lake and yard.

I hear a knock on the door and Maggie peeks in, "Hey we were all thinking of grilling out and jumping in the lake in a few minutes, you in?"

She walks into the room and closes the door behind her. "Are you okay? I know things are a little weird right now, but it will get easier."

I smile and shake my head yes. "Yea, I am fine, don't worry about me. Let me get my swimsuit on and I will meet you out there."

I recently bought a new swimsuit and if Darren wanted to play with my heart, then game on. I put on my swimsuit and a pair of cut-off jean shorts over top. The swimsuit cost me more than I would have liked but I'll admit I look good. It's like that one thing you buy, and it just fits so perfect that you wear it all the time and eventually it fades. Except you can't wear a swimsuit all the time so hopefully this will last me a while and I will get my monies worth out of it.

I put my sunglasses on top of my head and head out. I start to walk past the kitchen and stop. Wine sounds great and if I have to be here for the next 4 days with Amanda and Darren my ass is will be drinking the entire time. I pour myself a glass of white wine and take a big gulp. I fill my glass back up and walk out back to join everyone else.

The girls were sitting at the table talking and the guys were trying to turn on the grill.

"Wow, I love your swimsuit Tiff." Amanda takes off her sunglasses and agrees with Maggie. "Me too, it's so cute."

"Thanks, I just got it last weekend." Darren turns around and I can tell he likes it too.

I try not to smile at the effect I am having on him, so I take a sip of wine and sit down at the table. "I keep forgetting how pretty this place is."

Maggie smiles, "I know me too. We should come here more often, what do you think Ryan?"

"Absolutely. Maybe next time alone." Ryan walks towards Maggie and gives her a long kiss. Darren starts to whistle, and everyone starts to laugh. "Sorry everyone. Sometimes this woman makes it hard to resist her."

Amanda stands up and gets another beer out of the cooler. Okay let's go old school and play truth or dare. If you back out, you have to take a shot."

Wait what are we 13? What is she thinking? She can't honestly think that this could be a good idea. Playing truth or dare with this group of people is a death trap.

75

Everyone sits down around the table and Amanda speaks up, "Okay I'll go first, Maggie, truth or Dare."

Maggie smiles, "Truth."

"Okay, how is Ryan in bed?" Everyone starts laughing.

"Ryan is the best I ever had, and I do not have any complaints in that department!" Ryan and Maggie high five each other and blows air kisses at each other.

Ryan quickly jumps in, "Okay my turn. Darren. Truth or Dare man?"

Darren rubs his hands together and starts to laugh. "I pick Dare."

"Okay. I dare you to jump in the lake. Naked!" Darren stands up and downs the rest of his beer.

"Look man if you want to see my junk, all you had to do was ask." We all start laughing and Ryan starts whistling. Darren starts taking off his clothes and before I know it, he is butt ass naked. He starts running toward the lake and does a flip off the pier. If I haven't seen him naked before I would have been surprised at how ripped he is.

We all can't stop laughing and I am trying my best not to look at Darren as he gets out of the lake and walks towards us. Holy crap he is so hot. I mean I know he is hot but now with water dripping all over the place, all I can think of is... Crap what am I doing? I need to stop. As he gets closer, he starts to put his hand in front to cover himself. We all start to settle down and sit back in our chair just as he walks up. Maggie and Amanda have their back to him, and he uses the opportunity to give me a long lingering smile before I break eye contact and turn away.

Ryan sees the entire thing and gives me a wide grin. "Okay Darren it's your turn, who is the next victim?"

Darren is putting his clothes back on and calls my name. "Tiffany, Truth or Dare?"

I finish my glass of wine and smile, "Truth." This is going to be interesting.

"Okay, out of all the guys you have been with, who would you say was the best?"

Shit, he thinks he is so clever. "Well there was this guy I met when I was traveling to New Burn. We ran into each other a few weeks ago and we hooked up.

"OMG Tiffany, I didn't know that. That is so hot!" Amanda started hooting and hollering.

Darren stares at me and doesn't say a thing. He knows I was talking about him, but he can't say anything or take the credit.

"Alright, alright, Amanda, Truth or dare?" I try to move on and avoid eye contact as Darren sits down.

"Let's go with a dare." Amanda giggles. I didn't expect her to pick dare so now I need to think of something good.

"Okay, I dare you to shotgun a beer." She starts to moan and gets up to grab a beer from the cooler. The guys start chanting Amanda's name and she gets on her knees.

"Okay, one, two, three." Amanda starts gulping the beer and it's running down her chin. She is spilling more then she is drinking. When she finishes, she stands up and throws her arms in the air.

"Done bitches!" Everyone starts laughing. "Okay Ryan your turn. Truth or Dare?"

"Dare."

Amanda starts laughing, "Okay payback time. Let's see what I should make you do. I know! I dare you to play the rest of the game naked." We all look at Maggie to see if she is okay with it.

Maggie put her hands up like she is confused, "Why are you looking at me, she asked him to strip not me."

"Alright, get ready to see one of the wonders of the world." I spit out my drink and everyone starts laughing. Ryan stands up and starts taking off his clothes. I must say Ryan is not my type, but he definitely has a good-looking body.

Ryan spins around butt ass naked and says "Enjoy the view. Now Darren if you could go check on the burgers since I am naked, I would appreciate it man."

Darren walks over to the grill and starts plating the burgers. "Okay everything is ready." He puts all the burgers in the middle of the table, and we all start to dig in.

"Okay Tiffany, Truth or Dare. I take a huge bite of my burger and say Dare with a mouth full of food.

"I dare you to let Maggie take a shot off your stomach." I roll my eyes. I don't know what it is with guys and sisters.

"That's it, sure. Mag's choose your poison of choice." Maggie goes and fills up a shot of tequila and I lay down on the deck. Maggie straddles me and with just her mouth she takes a shot of tequila off my belly. Both guys are speechless. You can tell Amanda is annoyed that the spotlight doesn't include her. The guys start to stand up but Ryan forgetting he is naked quickly sits back down.

Amanda stands up and grabs the empty bottle of wine and lays it down on its side. "Okay let's make this more interesting. We have to now only do dare's and whoever the bottle lands on is who has to do the dare."

Since I was the last to get dared, it's my turn. "Okay I dare the next person to make out with the person sitting to their left. I spin the bottle and it lands on me. I go to reach for the bottle to spin again and Ryan yells.

"What are you doing?" You need to make out with Darren now. He gives me a devious look and I mouth that I hate him.

"Fine come on Darren." I go to stand, and I hear Amanda huff and say this is stupid.

Darren pulls me into his lap and kisses me. It starts as a sweet kiss on the lips but progresses quickly. He feels good and if it was up to him, he would continue making out right here. When we finally break apart, everyone is staring at us and although it did feel amazing, I immediately regret that I let Darren get his way.

Maggie feels the tension and tries to change the subject. "Okay let's clean up and think of something else to do. I can only handle so much of Truth or Dare in one night." I completely agree. I guess Amanda's little plan backfired and now she is pissed off.

I finish helping Maggie clean off the table and put the rest of the food back in the refrigerator. I can see Amanda still sitting outside pouting. Don't get me wrong I feel bad for the girl, but she did sleep with someone else too. I know she still has feelings for Darren, but they broke up and she has to stop acting jealous.

After everything is cleaned, I go into my bedroom and lock the door. I start the shower and make sure that the door that leads to Darren's bedroom is locked. I start to undress and just as I am about to get in the shower Darren opens his side of the bathroom door.

"Darren what the hell?" I grab my towel and try and cover-up. He starts to walk in and shuts the door behind him.

"What, it's nothing I haven't seen before." He walks toward me and takes the towel away and tosses it on the counter. "I can't stop thinking about that kiss earlier. You have me wrapped around you finger Tiffany."

He starts to kiss me again and quickly moves his way down my neck. I let out a loud moan and he tells me I need to be quiet.

"Darren, we can't. Amanda is in the other room." He picks me up and sits me on the counter.

"Shhh, don't make a sound." He continues to tease me by kissing my neck. He moves back up to my lips, gently kissing me until I can't take it anymore and I let out a little moan of frustration. Darren grabs my ass and pulls me to the edge of the counter. His touch is soft but the way he is taking control is just what I need. I can feel the temperature of my body start to rise and my breathing starts to increase.

"Darren, this isn't right. One minute you want to be friends, the next you are here kissing me. This is too confusing, and I can't keep going back and forth like this."

Darren moves his hand along my back and helps me down off the counter. I wrap the towel around me, and he leans forward and gives me another kiss on the lips before exiting the bathroom, "You are right Peaches, it isn't fair to you."

I stand there for a second before I realize the shower is still on. I jump in the shower and rinse off the smell of Darren. I take my time, not wanting to face everyone right now. As I lather up and rub the soap all over my body, I start to think of what just went on 5 minutes ago. God that was hot! The way he makes me feel. It's like my body needs him. And the more I have him the more I crave. He is like an addiction. Like a drug and I can't stop thinking about him.

I change into a pair of cut-off jean shorts and a tank top. I don't feel like blow drying my hair, so I let it air dry to get that beachy look. I apply a little bit of makeup and I am ready. Time to face everyone and get this night over with.

The night ends up not being too bad. We sit around playing cards, listening to music and singing. At around 10 pm the guys walk outside to start the fire pit and we pack up the cooler with beer. We all continue listening to music and talking about old times. Maggie, Amanda and I talk about high school, past relationships, old friends, and getting in trouble. It was nice and it almost made me forget about this weird triangle I am involved in.

Ryan and Maggie are the first to call it quits and head in for the night. Shortly after, Amanda calls it a night and Darren says he is going to stay and hang out a while longer.

"Are you heading in too?" Darren asks as he pops open another beer. I take a sip of my drink and shake my head no.

"No, I think I will stay up a little longer. I like sitting out on the pier at night, watching the lightning bugs glow across the lake."

"That sounds cool, want some company?" We both stand and walk toward the pier. I take my shoes off and dangle my legs over the edge. My toes just skim the water. He sits down next to me and does the same.

"Look, Tiffany, I am sorry about how everything turned out. I want to be with you, I do. God you have no idea how bad it kills me not to just kiss you when I want to. I am just afraid of how it will look, and I don't want Amanda to know we were together. Not yet anyway."

"I get it, I do. It just hurt when you told me you wanted me and then not even two days later you tell me you want to be friends. But I understand. The whole situation sucks." I take a deep breath and the pit in my stomach grows deeper. How can someone have this connection where it hurts to be away from them?

Darren finishes his beer and sits it down. "If I could change it though, I wouldn't. I think it is incredibly cool how we met. I haven't stopped thinking about those lips since the days we kissed."

I lean forward and kiss him, and he kisses me back. No matter how many times I feel his lips on mine, I don't think I will ever get enough of him.

"I don't think I could ever get tired of kissing you." Darren starts to move my hair to one side of my neck; his touch feels amazing. I am tingling all over and I arch my neck, so he knows to keep going. We are so in the moment, that we didn't hear anyone walk up to us. Someone starts to cough and we both freeze, afraid to look up, but we both know who is standing above us.

"Well that didn't take long did it?" Amanda is standing a few feet away when we both jump up. Darren is the first one to speak.

"Amanda, wait please." Amanda shakes her head and starts to walk back to the house. "You both can go to hell."

I sit with my head in my hands and start to cry. "This is exactly what we tried to prevent from happening. I am the worst friend in the world." I stand and start to walk away toward the house.

"Wait Tiffany, please. I am sorry. Let's at least talk about this." I stop and throw my hands in the air.

"What am I going to do now? I just lost a friend over this and we are not even in a relationship Darren. As far as I am concerned this is the worst thing that could have happened." I start to cry and turn around to walk away leaving Darren sitting on the pier alone. I fought every instinct I had not to turn around. Instead I went into my room and cried myself to sleep. I can't believe how much I just screwed things up for everyone. How am I going to explain to my sister that I just screwed over her best friend?

CHAPTER EIGHT

The next morning, I wake up before everyone else. The sun hasn't even come up yet and when I look at the clock it is only 5:15 am. I know I won't be able to fall back asleep, so I get up and get dressed. My mind keeps going over everything that happened last night while I make myself a cup of tea. It looks so pretty outside with the sun starting to rise so I decide to take advantage of this time and enjoy it before the house wakes up and all hell breaks loose.

I lean back on the chair and prop my legs up on the deck railing. I hold the cup of tea with both of my hands and take in how quiet it is outside. All I hear is the sounds of birds and the rustling of the trees. I forget how peaceful it is here. How did I get myself into this mess? I ruined a friendship all because I was into an unavailable guy. Boy can I sure pick them?

Let's revisit my history. First my high school boyfriend cheats on me. Everyone knew except me. But the best part was I didn't find out until we finally slept together. Then my fiancé that I met and dated all through college decides to sleep with my best friend and roommate. Now I fall for a guy who was unavailable and was dating my sister's best friend. I think I am cursed.

The back-patio door opens and closes, and I hear the faint sound of footsteps coming toward me.

"Tiffany, what are you doing out here alone?" I turn and see my sister try to cover her yawn.

I turn back around and stare at the lake, "I couldn't sleep. I have made so many bad choices over the last month. I honestly do not know what is wrong with me." I put my cup on the table and rub my face.

"Look nobody is perfect and I don't know what happened last night, but it will be okay. Do you want to talk about it?" Maggie has a concerned look on her face.

I roll my eyes and laugh a little. I don't know whether to be pissed because she is pretending, she doesn't know, or play into this. "You don't need to pretend you don't know Mags. I am sure Amanda told you what I did."

"I have no idea what you are talking about. Did you and Amanda get into a fight? She doesn't know about Darren, does she?"

I don't know how to begin to tell her, so I just take a deep breath and blurt it out, "Amanda caught me and Darren making out last night on the pier. God Maggie, Amanda was so upset. She took off before I could talk to her. I don't know what to do now?"

I am ashamed and the guilt is really starting to take a toll on me. I am not this type of person especially having gone through something recently with my ex-fiancé. I am better than this. I need to try and fix things before it's too late.

"Wow, I did not see that coming. Tiffany you need to talk to her and be honest. Maybe she will understand." Mags put her hand on my shoulder and gives me a sympathetic look.

"Would you understand? If I told you that your boyfriend met me on the road, we kissed and had this connection which led to this affair after running into him at my parents 4th of July party, would you understand?" I stand and walk over to the other end of the deck. I can't believe I am that girl. I look out toward the lake and remember when Maggie and I use to jump into the lake. We would spend all day playing. It was a much simpler time back then.

Maggie stands up and follows me to the other side of the deck, "Look you won't know if you don't talk to her, that's all I am saying."

The sliding glass door opens, and Amanda walks out. We both go silent, not sure what to say. "Tiffany, can I talk to you about last night?"

My eyes must have bugged out of my head because she starts to laugh. "Look, I don't want to fight, I just want to talk. We have known each other a while and even though I think you are a bitch right now; we have to figure this out. My best friend is your sister so it's not like we can go our separate ways."

Maggie walks back into the house to give us some privacy as we sit down at the table. "I guess I deserve that. Yea let's talk. Amanda you have to know that I never meant for this to happen. I did not know Darren was your Darren until......"

Amanda holds up her hand, "Wait what do you mean you didn't know he was my Darren? I introduced you to him as my

86

boyfriend Tiffany."

I shake my head, "Yes you did, but what I didn't tell you was I had already met him. On my way to New Bern my vehicle broke down. While I was waiting for it to get fixed, I met this guy in a bar and we hit it off. That was Darren. We both went our separate ways. I never expected to see him again but when you both showed up at my parents' house it freaked me out."

"So why did you keep it a secret that you two had already met each other then?" Amanda looks confused and then it hits her. "You guys hooked up the day you met on the road?"

I give her a guilty look. God, I feel so bad. "We kissed that's all and when he asked for my number, I said no. I never meant for it to go any further than this. I am so sorry. I did not mean to hurt you and I did not know he had a girlfriend at the time."

"Did you hook up with him after you found out?" Amanda is staring right at me. I know it is only 6 am but I could use a drink right about now.

"Yes, I did. I don't need to go into detail, but I also don't want to lie anymore. If I could take it back, I would. I never wanted to hurt you."

Amanda stands and starts pacing back and forth. "I never thought you would be capable of doing this to someone, but I guess I was wrong. Especially after you found Todd in bed with your best friend. I just thought we were starting to get close, but I guess I was wrong. Look Tiffany, I will be civil around you for Maggie's sake, but other than that, you are dead to me, got it?" Amanda turns around and walks back into the house.

I wait a few minutes to calm down and head back inside.

Everyone is standing in the kitchen talking about what they want for breakfast. This is so awkward, and I want to leave. I can't be here and have everyone keep staring at me. It's bad enough I hate myself right now, but I can't deal with everyone judging me.

After going back and forth, we all decided on pancakes and bacon. The guys start setting the table while I start to mix the batter and Maggie fry's up the bacon. Of course, Amanda just stands around sulking playing the victim. Occasionally, I see my sister glance over, giving her an, "I'm sorry" smile.

I hand my sister the bowl of mix and start the coffee. "Does everyone want coffee?" Everyone responds with a yes except Amanda. "Amanda would you like a cup?"

"Nope. Apparently, it's okay to share around here. If I want it, I will just have a taste of someone else's coffee." She doesn't look up from her nasty comment. She just turns around and sits down at the table.

My sister tries to change the subject. "So, I was thinking we can all go canoeing later." Nobody responds to her suggestion, and I honestly don't think she expected anyone to either. This was her way of having us each go to our corners until the next round starts.

After a few more flips in the pan, everything is done and is being placed on the table. We all sit and start to dig in. It's so quiet, you can hear everyone chewing.

Maggie has always hated silence and doesn't do well in awkward situations. She has always been like that, even when our parents fought when we were kids. I remember one time she purposefully acted like she fell down the stairs to get them to stop fighting. It worked too for a while until they started to catch on.

She tries to change the subject, "So Tiff, I forgot to tell you that I got a call from the storage unit asking when you are going to pick up your furniture?" Maggie continues to try and break the silence. Nobody is looking up from their plate and all you hear is chewing.

I start to laugh, "Yea I am not touching that crappy ass bedroom set. I will try and sell it, or maybe even give it away. I can't even look at it without envisioning Todd and her laying on the bed together."

"Yea I could only imagine. If you want me to help you get rid of it, I can." Maggie gives me a sympathetic smile. I know she regrets bringing this up.

"I just hate that he ruined it for me. I had that bedroom set since I moved out to Arizona for college. It was one of the first things I bought myself." I look down and start to move around the pancakes on my plate.

Ryan speaks up and offers to help me move it if I need it. "I have a big garage you can store your stuff in, just let me know."

I nod since I have a mouth full of pancakes and try to swallow the food before I'm ready to. "Thanks, Ryan, the set is still in good shape if anyone wants it."

Amanda laughs, "Right like anyone wants that hunk of junk bedroom set. One of the bedposts are loose."

I look at Amanda and roll my eyes, "You know what, you can go to hell, it's a nice set, and just because it's... wait you knew that? I never told you that."

Amanda starts to look at everyone nervously, "Yea I think you mentioned it a while back."

That doesn't make sense. Why would I tell her that? Amanda looks like she is starting to sweat a little.

Darren looks confused. "How could you have possibly known that Amanda?"

"Oh, shut the hell up Darren. I don't remember how I know, I just do." Amanda gives him the finger and he just laughs it off.

"Tiffany she probably saw it when we stayed at your apartment when we came to visit you last year, remember?" My sister is so sweet, but she is even more naive then Amanda is.

"Well then why did she say I told her when I didn't? Why not just say I remember seeing it when we came to visit? You know that still doesn't make sense. When were you in my room?"

Everyone has stopped eating and is staring at Amanda and me. She looks scared but finally puts down her fork.

"I was getting out of the shower when he walked through the door. He had a key, so I assumed it was okay he was there." Amanda is looking down at her plate.

"That doesn't make any sense though." Maggie looks worried and I can see her thinking about something. She turns to Amanda and Amanda just shakes her head just enough to worn Maggie to drop it.

I am the confused one now. "What is going on?" My voice is starting to tremble now.

"Okay Tiffany, calm down. It was a long time ago." Amanda looks scared and she starts looking at everyone to help her.

"What are you talking about it was a long time ago?" I can feel my hands start to sweat so I wipe them on my shorts.

"Okay remember when you took Maggie to see your office and I stayed at your apartment? Well, Todd came over to drop something off. I was getting out of the shower and it just happened."

"Wait, what?" I am shocked and I can't think clearly.

"We slept together okay... It meant nothing and he felt bad afterwards. He kept apologizing, saying it had been a long time since you guys had sex and......" Amanda starts crying and I stand up and start walking away.

"You bitch. You make me feel like the worst person alive for hooking up with Darren when you guys had only known each other for a little over 2 months, and you slept with my Finance? Get the fuck out of this house Amanda..... Now!"

Maggie stands up and puts her arms out to stop us from yelling, "Okay just wait, nobody is leaving. We all have known each other way too long to throw away this friendship."

CHAPTER NINE

I am furious and need to get away to clear my head. I need to go running. I go put on my shoes, grab my iPhone and walk outside. It's only 9 am so it is still cool outside, and I run better when it's not hot. As I walk away from the house, I put my earbuds in and hit play on Pandora. I start running as fast as I can, and I don't stop to look back. I run to the end of our street and turn toward the park. It's only about another mile down the road. I used to spend so much time at the park growing up when my parents took us here for the summer. Some of my best memories are in the park. My first kiss, the first time I finally did a cartwheel, the first time I tried beer.

I finally make it to the entrance and turn down the driveway that leads to the park. I can see that it's empty except an older couple walking their dog and a little boy and his dad fishing on the pier. I smile and walk toward the swings. I don't remember the last time I have been on the swings. My sister and I use to swing and jump off to see who landed the furthest away. I am surprised that we never broke anything. I sit down and start reminiscing about my childhood. My life growing up in this town was easy and safe. Much easier than it was before moving to Arizona for college.

I don't know how long I was swinging but it must have been a while. I look up and the older couple is already gone and so is the boy and his dad. I am the only one left in the park. It's quiet and comforting, but I know it's probably time to start heading back. I start to make my way out of the park when I feel a raindrop hit my cheek.

"Shit, this is just great." I look up and the sky is getting dark and the wind is starting to pick up. I look at my phone and I see that I have 5 missed calls and 7 text messages. They are from my sister and Darren, so I just ignore them and turn my phone back on silent mode.

I start to run back to the house and the raindrops start to pick up. I stick my phone inside my sports bra, so it doesn't get wet and tuck my headphones away too. This is going to be a long 2 miles back to the lake house. After 15 minutes I finally turn onto the main road and I know I still have about a mile left. I am now soaking wet and my shoes are starting to slip off making it hard to run. I start to slow down to catch my breath when I see an SUV driving toward me. The closer it gets I can tell its Ryan's SUV and Darren's driving. I roll my eyes and keep running. Why can't he get the hint and leave me alone?

"Hey, get in, you are going to get yourself sick." He rolls his window halfway down and waves me in.

I slow down keeping a fast pace, but I ignore him as if I

don't hear or see him. Darren has to stop and do a U-turn since he passed me, and I can hear him yelling from a few feet away. He's now driving next to me and yelling at me through the passenger side window and he looks pissed. "Please get into the damn vehicle Tiffany. You are soaking wet."

"Take a hint, Darren, I don't need you to save me. Leave me alone." I start to walk faster but he pulls off to the side of the road and jumps out.

"Tiffany stop! I don't know what your problem is, but we need to talk about this. Please get into the vehicle so I can take you home." He grabs my hand and I stop. I am so tired and cold that I want to give in, but I won't let myself.

"Darren please. I can't do this anymore. We can't do this back and forth thing. I am not yours to save." I can't even tell if I am crying because it is raining so hard. I push his hand off me and try and walk away again.

Darren grabs my arm and swings me around, so I am facing him now. He put's both of his hands on my shoulders to stop me from moving. "I know you are not mine Tiffany, but you should be. Ever since we met in that shit hole bar, I knew you were special. I know you were hurt by Todd, but you have to stop pushing me away."

"I can't do that. We bring out the worst in each other. I was with you when you were still with Amanda. I never wanted to be that person who cheats, but I am. I know what it's like to have my heartbroken and then I help you do that to Amanda." I am starting to shake now. I am so cold. My muscles are starting to ache because I am shaking so much.

"Look.... What we did while I was still with Amanda was wrong. I know that. But I also know that I couldn't let you get away from me again. I let you go the day we met, and we ended up meeting again at your parents. That must mean something to you and I promise it means something to me. We were given another chance to see if this thing we had is real. I am not giving that up until I know for sure."

I am speechless and I don't know what to say. Why couldn't he say these things to me before? My mind is going about a thousand miles a minute. Before I realize what I'm doing, I have my arms around him and we are kissing. He grabs my face with both hands, looks me in the eyes and puts his arms around me to stop me from shivering.

"Please let me take you back to the lake house. You are shivering and I don't want you to get sick." He grabs my hand and walks me to the passenger side of the SUV and opens my door. I slide inside and he shuts the door before too much rain gets in. He jogs over to the driver's side and jumps in. The SUV is warm and quiet. I sit back and close my eyes, just listening to the rain beat on the window. I can feel the SUV moving forward and I know we will be back at the lake house in no time at all. When we arrive, Darren helps me out of the vehicle and before I can take 5 steps toward the house, my sister in running out toward me looking worried.

"Oh, thank God you are back. I was so worried. Why didn't you answer any of my calls?"

I pull my phone out of my bra and toss it on the table. "I am sorry, I had it on silent, and then it started raining so I didn't want to get it wet."

Maggie can tell she shouldn't push me anymore then she already has with the questions. "Why don't you go take a shower and I will make you some hot chocolate with Kaluah."

I smile at my sister. It's one of those smiles that touch your eyes. She is always taking care of me. "Thanks, Maggie, that sounds great."

I walk to my room and shut the door. I have no idea what will happen with me and Darren and I don't know if I want anything to happen right now. For some reason I just feel numb to it all. I start to run my bath, making it extra hot so I can stay in the tub and relax for a while.

I flinch a little as I step inside the tub because of how hot it is. It feels really good though and it's exactly what I need. I start to lay back and before I know it, I am crying. I can't believe Todd cheated on me with Amanda. Now I know it was with two people, both who were close to me. How could I have been so naive to not see this? There had to of been red flags that I was not paying attention to. I was too caught up in my career, writing and trying to make a name for myself that I guess along the way I put everything else on the back burner. Maybe Todd was right when saying it was my fault.

After I wash my hair and my body I lay back and close my eyes. It's quiet and I'm enjoying this time to think and figure out what to do. I must have drifted off because the next thing I know I feel someone give me a soft kiss on the lips. When I open my eyes, Darren is sitting on the edge of the tub.

"I thought you might have fallen asleep in here. Are you ready to get out?" Darren has a towel already waiting for me.

"Yea thanks. I guess I did fall asleep. I needed that nap." I stand up in the tub and step over the side into the towel he is holding open. "Thank you."

"Look, I know you are not ready for a relationship right now. I mean you just found out that your asshole ex cheated on you with Amanda, but know I am not going anywhere. I wasn't lying when I said I want to see if there is anything more between us." Darren smiles and starts to exit the bathroom.

I shake my head before I turn and walk back into my room, closing the door. I get into my comfortable sweatpants and a tank top, brush my hair and put it in a messy bun on top of my head. I don't bother putting any makeup on. I can care less about how I look at the moment.

I leave my room and walk out to the living room where Darren, Maggie, and Ryan are sitting. I can smell the hot chocolate and it makes my mouth water. My sister points to my cup waiting for me on the coffee table. I grab it and curl up on the big armchair and take a sip, "Thank you, this taste really good Maggie."

Maggie smiles and takes a sip. "Tiffany, I know you don't want to, but we should all talk about what is going on here."

I smile because I knew this conversation was coming. I know she wouldn't let it go. "Okay, I guess I owe you that." I take another big sip of my hot chocolate and take a deep breath. "Okay so Pretty much Darren and I met when I was traveling back. You already know this. We hit it off and we didn't mean to go behind Amanda's back, honestly. I know it was wrong what we did. We tried to stop but somehow, we just kept ending back to where we started. The part that made me angry was I was beating myself up for what I did to Amanda when she slept with my ex-fiancé long before any of this. Then has the nerve to make me feel like shit."

"I know that was so messed up. When I found out I was so shocked. I hope you know that I had no idea, Tiffany." Maggie looked so sad.

"Of course, I know. Where is she anyways?" I am looking around the room and I don't see any sign of her things.

"I told her she needed to leave. I understand she is pissed but her sleeping with Todd when you guys were engaged was unforgivable." Maggie shakes her head and her eyes start tearing up.

"Maggie are you okay? You didn't have to make her leave. I know you guys are close."

Maggie puts her hands up to stop me. "Yes, we were close, but if she was really my friend, she wouldn't be able to do such a horrible thing to my sister. Our relationship can never be the same again."

I feel so bad about how everything turned out. Friends lost; secrets come out and feelings get hurt. I am relieved though. Everything is finally out in the open and there is nothing else to hide.

Ryan speaks up to lighten the mood a little. "So, I don't know if anyone wants to, but tonight the town is having a small carnival. You all want to go and drink some stale beer, eat fried dough and play some games?"

That actually sounds fun and I could use some distractions after this mess. Before nulling it over I am already agreeing to his plan. "Yes, that sounds like a lot of fun. Let's get some dinner first and then head over."

"Yes, bumper car time! I cannot wait!!!!!" Maggie starts to stand up and we all start laughing. Maggie has had this thing with bumper cars since we were kids. She loves them. I always pretended I hate them and let her drag me into the car, but I secretly like them too. She loves everything about carnivals, down to heckling the carnies at the game booths.

"Well alright it's a date then." We all stop and look at Darren, but he starts to laugh, "What, too soon?"

I smile at him and give him a wink. "Alright, it's a date!"

* * *

A few hours pass by and it almost six o'clock. I am getting ready and trying not to seem too nervous. I keep telling myself it's just a group of us going out, having fun and trying to stay away from the drama. Keeping it simple, I put on a pair of jean shorts, a black halter top and flip flops. I curled my hair and I am keeping it down but to make it more casual I put my sunglasses on my head that I can also use as a makeshift headband. I am just about done when I hear someone knocking on my door. I take a deep breath and glance in the mirror one last time. Here goes nothing.

"Hey, it's Darren, you almost ready?" He starts to open the door and peeks in with his hand covering his eyes. "Are you decent?"

I start to laugh, now he wants to be a gentleman. "Yes, I am ready to go in just a sec, I am looking for my wristlet, so I don't have to carry my purse."

He opens his eyes and smiles, "You look really pretty

Peaches." He enters the room and sits on the bed, "What does the wrist thing look like?"

"It's about the size of my phone and looks like a wallet with a handle. It's black and grey. Now that I think about it, I might have forgotten to pack it." Damn I didn't want to carry around a purse tonight.

"That's okay, I can hold your stuff if you want. Give me what you were going to bring, and I'll put it in my wallet." Darren is holding out his hand waiting.

"Are you sure you don't mind, that would be awesome?" I start to open my wallet to take out my photo ID, credit card and twenty dollars in cash and hand it to him. I put my phone in my back pocket.

"Alright then, I am all set. Thank you." I smile and hold out my hand for him to stand up from the bed and leave. We both are heading toward the door when he stops.

"Hey, just in case I don't get to tell you tonight, thank you for agreeing to go out tonight. Date or not, this will be fun." Darren holds my hand and smiles at me.

My stomach dropped and now I have butterflies. I can't believe how much of an effect he has on me.

We all arrive at Café Lugano's, an Italian restaurant. Soon as we get out of the car, we can smell the food and my stomach rumbles. At least I am getting my appetite back. "Oh gosh this place smells so freaking good!"

Darren grabs my hand and we all start to walk inside. Something about the way he holds my hand makes it feel right. Like everything will be okay. I decided right there to just enjoy myself

100

and go with it. No pressure or expectations, just fun. I need to start thinking about myself and what I want. Not what I am afraid people will think.

I stop walking for a second and Darren stops too, wondering what's wrong. "Hey, can you two grab us a table I need to talk to Darren for a second outside."

My sister has a concerned look on her face, but I smile to let her know everything is okay. Darren and I walk back outside so we have privacy.

"Everything okay? Is this because I said you smell good when we got out of the vehicle?" He leans his back against the wall of the restaurant.

I start laughing and I walk toward him. I press my hands lightly on his chest, standing on my tippy toes and kiss him on the lips. "I just want to say thank you for being cool with everything."

I break away and he grabs my hand and holds it on his chest. I can feel his heart pounding. "This is what you do to me." He smiles and looks right into my eyes. The way he looks at me is incredible. He doesn't have to say or do anything, just the look alone has my stomach in knots and my heart pounding.

We find our table inside the restaurant and sit down. "Alright who wants to split a bottle of wine with me?" Maggie says she already ordered a beer and so did Ryan. Damn, I know I can't drink an entire bottle myself.

"I'll drink wine with you. Red or white?" He is looking at the wine list when the waiter comes over to take our order.

After we order our drinks and food, we are all talking and laughing. I am really enjoying myself and I can't believe how easy this is. We all get along so well and it feels like we have been friends forever. The food finally arrives, and we dig in. I ordered lasagne and it's amazing. Darren and Maggie both ordered chicken alfredo and Ryan ordered chicken parmesan.

Darren pours us both another glass of wine while we finish up our meal and the waiter comes by to see if we want dessert, but we all pass knowing we will get something at the carnival soon. After the guys pay the bill, we all leave and start to walk across the street to the carnival. It's now getting dark and we can see the carnival all lit up. I always think going at night is way more fun because of all the lights. It's just not the same during the day.

While we are standing in line at the ticket booth, we are trying to decide what to do for tickets. "I think we should all just get a wristband. Its unlimited rides and one free drink."

"Yea I agree, it seems like the better deal. That gives us four hours of unlimited fun." Maggie is starting to get excited. She can't standstill. Carnivals bring out the child in her. It's so funny to see her like this.

We get our wristband and walk inside. Ryan suggests doing the Ferris wheel first since its closest to us. While we wait in line Maggie and I start laughing at the little boy in front of us. He has a ring of chocolate around his mouth and he is just staring at the Ferris wheel in amazement. I love how innocent kids are. Not a care in the world. I look back at Darren and see him and Ryan whispering about something. When Ryan sees me, he stops and nudges Darren.

It's our turn so Darren holds my waist and guides me up the ramp to sit in the cart. The guy closes the lap bar and it moves forward so Ryan and Maggie can get in. "So, what were you whispering about earlier?"

Darren smiles at me and leans forward. "You'll see soon enough babe." I look at him and wonder what he is up to.
We are almost at the top and I turn around to look down at Ryan and my sister in the cart below us.

I gasp at what I am seeing and then the Ferris wheel stops. Ryan is proposing to my sister. He has the ring out holding the box open and he is talking. I can't hear anything, but I can only imagine what is being said right now. Next thing you know fireworks are going off and we can hear people below cheering. "Did you know about this?"

Darren starts laughing. "Yea, Ryan had this whole thing planned out for a few weeks now. I look back down and see Ryan putting the ring on Maggie's finger. She is crying and laughing. They both start kissing each other. "Woohoo! Congrats, I love you both so much!" They break away and start laughing.

Maggie is grinning ear to ear. I can tell she is so happy. "I'm engaged!" Everyone starts cheering again and the Ferris wheel starts to head toward the ground.

My baby sister is engaged. Wow! I knew this would happen, but I didn't think it would be this weekend. We have talked about getting married since we were little. We would play wedding in the backyard, pulling flowers out of our mother's garden to make bouquets and stealing tasty cakes out of the pantry to use for our wedding cake. And now its officially here. Maggie is getting married! Darren and I get off the ride first which is perfect so I can take their picture.

I take a few quick snaps and run up to Maggie and Ryan giving them both a hug. "I am so happy for you guys." I look at my sister and smile. I can't believe she is going to get married.

"Thank you, Tiffany. I love you too. I am so freaking excited right now." Maggie has this happy twinkle in her eye and Ryan looks like he just won the lottery and in my eyes they both did. I am glad they found each other.

We continue riding rides and playing games for the next few hours before heading home. This night was exactly what I needed, being a part of good news and having fun with my friends and family. In a way it was like I was starting over again, but this time I won't make the same mistakes.

CHAPTER TEN

The next few weeks are a blur. Maggie has been talking non-stop about wedding details and Darren and I have been spending pretty much all our time together. I never would have guessed things would have escalated this fast between us.

I am walking across the beach, holding Darren's hand. It's such a beautiful day. The breeze is perfect, the sun is just starting to set and we are all alone. I don't see anyone on site. I lean in and kiss him. I feel Darren run his fingers down my arm and onto my lower back. Darren reaches down and starts playing with the waistline of my shorts before moving to the front to unbutton them. Without any warning a loud ringing starts going off and startles both of us.

Fuck! I reach over and grab my phone off the nightstand. Another sex dream, really? I grab the pillow and throw it across the room. I am so horny and sex-crazed lately. I cannot get enough of Darren and I'm pretty sure he is starting to think there is something wrong with me.

"Hey babe, good morning..." I say, trying to sound like I have been up for a while.

'Hey good morning. So, I woke you up, huh?" I rolled my eyes as I swung my legs over the bed to get up.

"No, why would you think that?" I am covering the phone while I pee and brush my teeth. The last thing I need him to know is he is right. He is ALWAYS right and loves to rub it in my face.

"Oh, I don't know because it's 9 am and you told me to come to pick you up at 8:30 am."

I stop dead in my track. Shit. Is it really that late? Sure enough, I look at my phone at its almost 9 am. I start to smell coffee and I take a deep breath.

"And yes, I made you coffee. Hurry up and get ready. I'll have a cup waiting for you." I can hear Darren end the call so I throw the phone on the bed and head toward my closet to pick out something to wear.

I am almost finished getting ready but I need coffee so I head out to the living room where I see Darren sitting on the porch talking to someone on the phone. I pour myself a cup of coffee and check my email and Facebook while I wait for him. I keep glancing out onto the patio; I can't help wondering if everything is okay. He looks tired and annoyed for some reason. Who could he be talking to?

After a few minutes he ends the call and comes back inside. He smiles at me as he is walking toward me but I can sense there is something wrong. He has the worst poker face when it comes to hiding his feelings.

"Hey are you okay?" I ask as I take a sip of my coffee.

Darren nods and walks into the kitchen avoiding eye contact at all cost.

"Yea I'm good. Just work stuff. Hey so I am thinking that we should start planning the bachelor/bachelorette parties. What do you think?"

I feel like something is off. Like he is changing the subject to get me to forget his weird phone call. "Sure, that's fine with me but it is kind of early. We don't know the details yet."

Darren walks back toward me, "Okay, just let me know when I should be planning it. I don't want to drop the ball or anything."

I finish my coffee and rinse out the cup before putting it in the dishwasher. As I leave to finish getting ready, Darren stops me and hugs me. "I am so happy we were able to put everything behind us." He kisses me and I kiss him back. It's one of those soft, but sexual kisses that you feel throughout your body. I break away and head toward my bedroom. If I stay there, I know we will never leave the house.

I finish my makeup and grab my purse. I hear him talking again to someone else as I approach the living room. It's really low, but I can make out a few words.

"I am not giving you any more money Jess. I gave you enough the other night." He hangs up the phone and turns around to me see staring at him. I don't give him a chance to explain. I knew it. I knew something was off. I start to back away and walk toward the bedroom. Before I get the chance to close the door all the way, he pushes it open and I stumble backward.

Darren catches me so I don't fall. I almost appreciate that

107

but quickly start hitting him to let me go. He grabs both of my hands and pushes me toward my bed. I can feel the side of the mattress against the back of my legs and it makes me fall back on the bed. Darren lays on top of me and pins my arms down so I can't hit him anymore.

"Stop. Babe please stop and let me explain. Fuck!" He looks really scared and he should be. Enough is enough.

I start to cry and scream, "Get off me Darren. I hate you." I can't control my tears and they are already soaking the sides of my face and running down my jawline.

"Tiffany, please you don't know what you overheard. That was my ex-girlfriend. She is back in town and she keeps calling me. What you overheard was me telling her to leave me alone. She keeps asking me for money and telling me she wants to get back with me but we have been done for over a year now. I promise you I want nothing to do with her."

I stop moving and look at Darren. I am trying to read him to see if he is telling me the truth.

Darren doesn't let me speak. He kisses me with a forceful kiss and that stops me from trying to get free of Darren's hold.

"Do you think I would jeopardize the chance of losing you again?" He starts to kiss me again and I wrap my legs around his back letting him know that this is okay.

"I will never hurt you Tiffany. One of these days you will realize that I am not lying to you and the past is in the past."

I shake my head and lean toward him. "I know, I just got scared. I keep thinking that what we have is too good to be true."

I go into the bathroom and clean myself up. I wash my face

and reapply my makeup before brushing my hair. I take a deep breath before walking back out into the bedroom where Darren is waiting me for.

Ten minutes later we are both walking out the door, prepared to meet Maggie and Ryan for brunch like nothing ever happened. We are helping them with some of the wedding stuff, discussing dates, locations, colors, etc. All the stuff that you would typically do.

The drive to the restaurant is quiet. I don't think Darren or I know what to say to each other. Do I believe him? Do I give him the benefit of the doubt? I mean there is no reason I shouldn't trust him. He has been completely honest with me. I start to have a debate in my head and before I know it, we are at the restaurant and he is staring at me, trying to figure out what's going on in my head.

Darren reaches for my hand and brings it to his lips, kissing my hand and placing it against his chest, "Tiffany, I promise, you are the only one on my mind all the time. The only one I want to be with. She tends to reach out to me when one of her current relationships end. She usually stops calling after I tell her no a few times."

I smile and reach forward, giving him a soft kiss on the lips, "Thank you, babe. I needed to hear that again."

I feel better walking up to the restaurant. I'm glad this is all cleared up and I can now give my sister my full attention. Maggie and Ryan are already sitting down. They have ordered a round of mimosas already for everyone.

"Hey love birds.... Thanks for getting the round of drinks to start us off." I smile and sit down, picking up my glass and taking a sip.

Over the next two hours, Maggie has gone over everything you could think of that relates to a wedding. I am trying to act like I am interested in everything but talking about this nonstop for hours is mentally exhausting. I start to play with my napkin, folding it in all different ways, wondering how restaurants made it look so nice.

Maggie immediately gets my attention and I snap back into reality when I hear her squealing with excitement. "Alright so now Tiffany and I are going dress shopping until 2 pm. What do you guys have planned?"

They both look at each other, trying to figure out if they want to tell us the truth or not. Ryan speaks up, "We are going to just head back to Tiffany's apartment and hang out until you ladies are done."

"So pretty much you guys are going to play Call of Duty for the next few hours and drink." Maggie rolls her eyes and we all stand up to walk outside.

"See sweetheart, it's crazy how well you know me already and we are not even married yet." Maggie laughs and gives Ryan a kiss and a hug before we all go our separate way for the next few hours.

* * *

Twenty minutes later Maggie and I enter a bridal boutique downtown. It's so fancy inside and I feel underdressed and judged. It's one of the stores that require an appointment and doesn't take walk-ins, not even to browse. Everything is white, cream and mauve.

Giant overstuffed chairs sit in the middle of the store. They probably think that the majority of people who sit in them are waiting for two or more hours while they watch dress after dress being pranced around and admired.

Since when was my sister this boujee.... She never cared about stuff like this. I try to play along and be a supportive sister. The last thing I want is her to go all bridezilla on me, especially in a store like this.

We sit down on a round posh chair surrounded by mirrors. The sales lady greets us and hands both of us a glass of champagne. Okay maybe this isn't that bad. I mean, I do like champagne. Maggie starts telling the sales lady the style of dress she is interested in, showing her pictures off her phone and before you know it, they have about 10 dresses ready for her to try on. The first dress Maggie tried on was a sweetheart style dress. It was off white and it bunched up on the side. It was beautiful but it wasn't her style.

After four more dresses and 2 more glasses of champagne, Maggie came out wearing a mermaid style dress. It has a beautifully beaded belt right under her breast and it was open in the back. The dress was all satin and had an off-white tint to it. It was amazing and it complimented her very well. This was the dress and I could tell she thought it was too.

"Maggie, you look beautiful. Do you like it?" I start to tear up. I still can't believe my baby sister is getting married.

"Tiffany, this is the one. I love it. I feel beautiful and sexy in this dress. Take a picture. Mom wasn't feeling well so I told her I would send her a picture of the dress if I find it." Maggie is all smiles. I know Ryan will be too when he sees her in this dress. The sales lady checks on us and asks how we are doing. Maggie tells her we have a winner and spins around for the sales lady to take a look and see if any alterations need to be done. I take a few more pictures before she takes off the dress and hands it to the lady to pack up.

I start to pack up our stuff and quickly send our mom a few of the pictures when Maggie walks out of the dressing room. I hear her on the phone with Ryan. She is so excited to tell him she found the dress of her dreams. I stop and just watch her talk to Ryan on the phone. Her facial expressions when she talks to him and the way she smiles has me smiling. I start thinking about how this was almost me a year ago and I was in her shoes doing this very thing. But I never smiled like that, and honestly, I don't remember ever being that happy when I was trying on wedding dresses.

I quickly shake out of it and realize Maggie is now checking out and making the appt to get her dress sized. "Alright I think that should do it Tiffany. I have everything I need. Let's go home to our guys." She smiles and thanks the sales lady for helping her and I grab my purse. This shopping experience was a lot better than anticipated but I am ready to call it a day and relax.

A few minutes later we are entering my apartment to the guys playing Call of Duty. They are both sitting on the living room floor, Indian style, looking like children. It's adorable. Darren looks up and smiles giving me a little wink before returning his focus to the game. Right there all my hesitation and doubt go out the window. It's crazy how one look from him can make me feel at ease. I haven't told him yet, but I am starting to fall for Darren Hart.

CHAPTER ELEVEN

Over the next month, Darren has slept over almost every night. He wakes up, gets ready, goes to work and when he returns from work, we cook dinner together and watch tv until we fall asleep in each other's arms. He helps me do laundry and we even have fun going to the grocery store together. I never would have guessed how much fun playing house would be with him.

Since I am a freelance writer that works from home, at times I get stir crazy, catching myself constantly checking the clock to see if it is almost time for him to come home. I count down the hours. I am so happy right now that I even have inspiration which helps me in my writing. Everything is working out great. I am ahead of my deadlines and have turned in all my articles to my editor. I start to pack up my laptop and put away my notes when I realize I haven't stopped smiling. Then the idea pops in my head. I know it is crazy but he practically lives with me anyways now. Tonight, I am going to ask Darren to move in with me. This is a big step and we haven't been seeing each other for too long but something just feels right. Normally I would be freaked out but I am weirdly excited about this.

I pour two glasses of wine and wait for Darren to come home from work. I am starting to get a little antsy so I down my glass and pour myself another. Liquid courage is what I need. I hear the rattling of keys and my heart leaps. I take both glasses and meet Darren in the living room.

"Hey, babe, welcome home. How was your day?" I smile and we both lean forward to give each other a quick kiss. I love how comfortable this is and that we have a routine, it feels normal.

"Hey beautiful. Is one of those glasses for me?" He laughs and I hand him the glass of wine. As he takes a sip, and starts emptying his pockets, removing his wallet and keys. I watch him take off his shoes before he realizes I am staring at him.

"What's up my creepy girlfriend? Why are you watching me like a hawk?" Darren takes another sip and starts to walk towards me sitting on the couch.

"Darren, I wanted to talk to you about something." I make a motion for him to come sit down next to me. I am on the edge of my seat and I know I am not hiding it well that I am nervous.

"Tiffany are you okay? You look sick..." He puts his wine glass down and turns to me.

"Yes, I am fine. I just wanted to talk to you about our living arrangements."

Darren looks worried. "Look I know I have been staying here a lot lately. I am sorry, I just want to be with you all the time. I can start staying the night at my place if you need someplace."

I am speechless. He really thinks I want him to go. "No, no, Darren, I want the opposite. I was going to ask you if you wanted to move in with me."

He stops and stares at me before a huge grin comes across his face. "Are you sure? You want us to live together officially?"

I look puzzled. Does he think this is too fast? "Yes, I do. I love being with you Darren. If you are not ready that's fine. I just thought that since we spend all our time together, maybe we should consider the idea."

"Peaches, I would like nothing more than to move in with you, to wake up with you each morning and see that crazy bed hair of yours." He leans forward and kisses my lips.

God, I can't get enough of him. I move closer and put each leg over his, straddling him on the couch.

Darren starts to rub my back and we both start kissing, finding a rhythm that works for both of us. He feels good and I want more. I grab the bottom of my shirt and pull it over my head as I stare at him, those eyes are hypnotic. I lean forward to kiss him again; I can feel Darren grab my ass, pulling me on top of him. God, I love this man. The things he does and the way he makes me feel is amazing. He unclasps my bra and pulls it slowly down my arms as he lightly kisses and brushes his lips along my collar bone and down my arm.

I want Darren. Not just physically but emotionally. That connection we have, I crave and right now I don't think I can ever get enough of him. He makes me feel like I can't live without him. Being with Darren and sharing the connection we have together is the thing I honestly crave the most. It's never been like that with anyone else. I move faster and faster and I can't control my breathing. I finally have my release, but I know he hasn't yet. I keep moving up and down while kissing him and about a minute later I can tell he's there. He grabs the back of my head and has a hand full of hair when he finishes. I start to slow down and he lets my hair go, kissing the side of my neck. I almost forget where I am. All I can think about is how lucky I am. A few months ago, I felt like I wanted to die. My world completely changed and now I can't imagine my life being anything but this. Everything happens for a reason and while it sucked having to of had witnessed my fiancé with someone else, if I had to choose it all over again, I would go through that pain to get to where I am today with Darren.

* * *

The next day Darren officially starts to move in his stuff. I woke up to boxes everywhere. I walk out into the living room and yawn, "Hey, how long have you been up? It's only 10 a.m." There are boxes everywhere. My apartment looks trashed and my anxiety starts. I quietly tell myself to calm down and smile, not wanting to ruin today.

Darren looks up from rummaging through one of the boxes and smiles with that sexy grin he has. "Hey there, don't you look cute this morning. I have been up since 6 a.m. I couldn't sleep so I went and got some of the boxes from my apartment that I didn't unpack yet. I hope that was okay."

I pour myself a cup of coffee and sit down on the couch.

"Of course, that's fine. Do you need any help?"

"Yea, actually later do you want to come back to my apartment and help me pack some of my stuff and we can get lunch while we are out." Darren has the goofiest smile. You can tell he is excited about moving in with me and I hope this works out for the best. I can't take any more heartache.

"Yea, that sounds good. Soon as I finish my coffee, I'll get dressed and start clearing out some space in my closet for you." I blow Darren a kiss and walk back into my room. I didn't even think about where all his stuff was going to go when I asked him to move in. I open my closet door and look around, it's so organized, and there is a spot for everything. Now I am going to have to share it. Crap. I wonder how he feels about using the hall closet. A couple of hours later the closet has been reorganized and there is room for all of Darren's stuff. I can't believe I made this work. I stand back and admire my handy work.

"Darren, come here and look at what I did." I am laughing when he walks in. I am proud of myself. I feel like a little kid that wants praise from their parents for picking up their toys.

"Wow, you must really love me to give me half your closet space." He starts tickling me and I run out of the room.

"Okay, okay... let's go get some lunch. I am starving and we need to get the rest of your stuff anyways."

Darren treats us to lunch at Karra's Café down the street. It was good, and I can see that being my new favorite place. The sandwiches all come with this amazing house dressing and homemade chips. The place is small inside, not many places to sit down and eat, but the food was well worth it.

After lunch we go to Darren's apartment and I am happy to see that he is clean and organized. That means I won't have to pick up after him like I am his personal maid. I can't believe I never saw his place before this. Most of his stuff is already inboxes. He doesn't have much furniture and it's a studio apartment, so pretty much what I see is here. He has a few bar stools at the counter, a bedroom set, entertainment stand, and a few dressers. Should that worry me that this is the first I am seeing his place and we are moving in together? Maybe we are rushing things. I feel like I have an angel on one shoulder telling me to use my head and be logical, and on the other shoulder I have a devil that tells me to forget all my instincts and go for it. His apartment and building are nice. I know it is way out of my price range and even though it's a studio, it's a lot bigger.

I hear Darren cough a few times and I look up at him staring at me. I guess I was in my head longer than I thought. "I'm sorry, did you say something?"

"Tiffany is everything okay? Are you positive you are good with us moving in together?" Darren puts down a box and walks toward me.

"Yes, I am fine. I was just daydreaming. Nothing to worry about. Will you be able to end your lease on the apartment?" I smile and hope this is good enough so he will change the subject.

"Okay good, and this is a condo I own so I will probably just rent it out. But anyway, I was just saying this bed folds into a couch that we can probably fit in the office and I can bring the barstools since you don't have any." Darren stands stand looking around the room to see if he forgot to mention anything.

Oh wow, I didn't realize he owned this place. "Yea, I think

that will work. One of the dressers can fit in the corner of the bedroom, and if you want the nightstands that can fit in the closet." I smile and he walks towards me. He grabs my hips so I can't move, and he kisses me. How could moving in with this man be so wrong, when this feels so right?

Within minutes he has me sitting on his counter and we are making out like high school kids. I love this new phase in the relationship where we can't keep our hands off each other. Those butterflies you get when they look at you a certain way. He leans forward to kiss me on my cheek and he whispers, "I can't wait to do that anytime I want Peaches."

I am head over heels for this man and all I can formulate to say is, "Uh-huh". I am still coming down from my make-out session with Darren. I need to get away from him or we will never get any work done. I jump down from the counter and head into the kitchen to make sure we didn't leave anything.

Darren starts to grab some boxes from the room, "I'll be back, I am going to start running these down to my truck."

While he is downstairs, I use his bathroom to clean up and I catch a glimpse of myself in the mirror. Who is this person? She looks happy, satisfied, and excited. I love this new version of me. She is energetic and looks alive! I think she is here to stay for the long haul.

After a few hours we are finished packing up his apartment and start heading back to my apartment, or should I say our apartment. This is going to take some time to get used to this. I pull out my phone and call my sister.

"Maggie, hey, what are you up to? I wanted to see if you and

Ryan wanted to come over for dinner tonight? Perfect, we will see you guys around 7 p.m. then, okay?" I smile and put my phone back into my purse.

"So, you are going to tell Maggie and Ryan we are now living together by inviting them over to dinner?" He is laughing and shaking his head.

"I thought it would be a fun way to tell them. Is that okay?" I suddenly stop and realize I didn't ask him. Crap.

"Yea that's fine. I am just giving you a hard time." Darren pulls up outside our apartment and smiles. "Home sweet home Peaches."

I jump out of the truck and we both quickly start to unload everything. Over the next few hours we were able to get everything moved in and almost put away. Darren had plenty of space in our closet since I made room, and the furniture he brought over fit perfectly once we rearranged some stuff. The barstools were the perfect touch to complete the dining area and the couch looks nice in the office. I can't believe this actually worked out.

We are both exhausted and neither of us want to make dinner tonight. I crack open the bathroom door, "Okay, so how about we order the family meal from Ricardo's down the street? It comes with an entire rotisserie chicken, bread, two sides and a dessert."

Darren yells out from the shower, "Yea babe that sounds perfect. If you place the order, I can go pick it up and grab some wine while you finish getting ready. They should be here in an hour."

Soon as Darren gets out of the shower, I jump in to clean up and notice Darren added his bathroom stuff with mine. His razor is standing in the cup with mine, he has his loofah hanging from the hook and a special men's body wash sitting on the shelf. It makes me smile. I open the cap and smell his body wash. Yup, that is the smell, every time I hug Darren, I smell this and now I know what it is and I love it.

Darren yells that he is leaving to get the food and wine. Crap, I am running late. I turn off the shower and dry off when I hear him leave and lock the door. A few minutes later I am rummaging through my closet to find something to wear when I hear the front door handle jiggle. Darren must have forgotten his keys. I yell for him to hold on, and I run to the door to let him in, but he isn't there. That's weird. I swear I heard someone at the door. After I close and lock it back up, I finish getting ready. Darren Should be back shortly and Maggie and Ryan should be here in 20 minutes.

Within 10 minutes I hear Darren opening the front door and inviting them into our apartment. Everyone is exchanging hello's and making conversation. Maggie asks where I am, and Ryan starts talking about the new Call of Duty game that just got released.

I hear my sister yell from the living room, "Tiffany, your apartment looks different. What did you do?"

I turn the corner and smile, "Well our apartment looks different because we moved in Darren's stuff today."

There is silence for a second, and Ryan speaks first. "Holy crap that's awesome you two. Let's cheers to that."

Maggie grabs her glass and hands me the other one sitting on the counter and we all clink our glasses and cheers. "I can't believe you guys are living together. That's a big step."

I can tell Maggie is trying to read me and figure out if I am okay with this. She is my little sister, yet she seems to be the one taking care of me. I give Maggie a quick wink, so she knows everything is fine. "Yea we are excited. Okay so let me get dinner set up for everyone, it shouldn't be too much longer." This was the way to host a dinner party. Everything even comes in pretty to-go containers, so I don't have to do much but sit out the plates and silverware.

The dinner was nice. Maggie tells us how our parents are driving her crazy with the wedding stuff and Ryan stays quiet and lets Maggie vent. He doesn't say one word but just listens and nods when it is appropriate. It's cute that he is letting herb blow off steam and not try to fix the situation. He really knows my sister. I admire them both.

After dinner we all get more wine and we start talking about the possible honeymoon ideas over dessert. Maggie wants to go to Hawaii and Ryan wants to do a cruise and travel to a few different places. I sort of agree with his idea. I am always down for a cruise. You don't have to worry about driving or what to do each night. They plan everything out; the only decision is which day to do what. It's so convenient.

That night while we get ready for bed, Darren asks if I am okay. He climbs into bed and gets comfortable but doesn't take his eyes off me.

"Yeah why wouldn't I be?" I smile and finish rubbing lotion on my arms. He has good intuition for a guy. This could be interesting. I never had a relationship with a man who can sense when something was wrong.

"You just seem like you have something on your mind. Ever since you and your sister started talking about the wedding at dinner."

"Oh, it's just there are so many details and stuff to do. My head is spinning, that's all. I can only imagine how she feels." I smile and lean over to kiss him.

Darren kisses me back. "Oh okay, because you know we will have what they have at some point too. So, if that was what you were worried about, you shouldn't worry. I love you and I am here for the long haul. You do not need to worry about that."

I am shocked. Is he seriously telling me what I think he is? How can he read me so well? We have only known each other for a few months but it's like he has known me years.

"I know Darren. I love you too. We will have our day, someday. I know that. I just want to enjoy what we have now. There is absolutely no rush, let's just enjoy it."

I give him another kiss; say goodnight and I turn out the light. The first night sleeping together in our apartment feels amazing. Falling asleep in his arms was exactly what I needed. The reassurance that we are going down the right path and he feels the same way as I do is all that I need.

CHAPTER TWELVE

I have started adapting to my new living arrangement and the last few weeks have flown by. It was never this easy when I lived with my ex. He always criticized me for everything, put me down any chance he got, and yet somehow, he made me feel like I needed him. At the time I didn't realize that. I thought we had the best relationship. My friends all envied me and always told me how lucky I was. This included the friend that was sleeping with my ex. Funny how things work out, but our relationship wasn't honest. It was fake, like a tv show. I let everyone see the best parts and not the reality of it all. That was my fault but now things are different and I won't make that mistake again. I am sure of that!

Now that I think of it, I don't even know what happened to them. After I caught Todd and Julie together in my bed, I shut down. I blocked their numbers, unfriended them on Facebook, and removed myself from their life completely. For all I know they could still be together. I don't care though. They both deserve each other. I just don't know how someone who says they love you can hurt you that much and do horrible things to you.

I hear a car horn beep and it brings me back to reality. I realize I am staring out the window and not writing. I have an article due tomorrow and I am only halfway done. I re-pour myself another cup of coffee, sit down in front of my computer and give myself a pep talk. Okay Tiffany, time to focus so you can complete this article. I take a sip and start typing away. By noon, I have everything typed and now I only need to proofread it. I can't believe how easy this topic came to me.

My editor wanted an article about starting over, relocating, life changes, and how to evaluate if relocating for a job is right for you. I don't know why I am so surprised. I relocated myself not too long ago, but it was for completely different reasons. I guess it doesn't really matter why. Relocating takes the same type of energy regardless of the reason.

I put the finishing touch on my article and I am pleased with how it turned out. I save it and email it to my editor. Within 10 minutes he responds that it's perfect and I did a great job. A huge smile crosses my face. I love getting praised for my work. It's better than anything. That satisfaction that something I created is good and others enjoy it, nothing can beat that.

It's so different here in New Bern. My friends, my boss, everyone here treats me differently. This is just the reassurance that I need to show that I am making the right move. It was time to come back home and start over. And I am starting to see that now.

I am meeting Maggie for a late lunch to discuss some more wedding details. She is getting so excited and everything seems to be finally coming together. After I finish getting ready, I head out of my apartment but something stops me dead in my tracks. There is a bouquet sitting at my door. That's odd. Most flower delivery companies knock and have you sign for the flowers. I pick up the flowers and head back into the apartment so I can put them on the counter. I grab the card to see who the flowers are from but the only thing written on the card is *I need you*!

Who could have sent me this? If it was Darren, I feel like it would have said it was from him. Something just seems off. I lay the card on the counter and leave the apartment. The restaurant is only a few blocks over so I decide to walk. It helps me clear my head and by the time I get to the restaurant, I already forgot about the flowers.

I see Maggie already sitting down at the table, so I head over to her, "Hey Mag's, I hope you haven't been waiting long." We hug and Maggie shakes her head no.

"No, I just got here like 3 minutes ago. Don't worry. Oh, I ordered us a round of mimosas." She is smiling from ear to ear.

"Sounds perfect. So, what is on the agenda today? Did you pick a date yet? We can't book anything until a date is picked." I look through the menu while I listen to Maggie giving me the most recent updates on her plans.

The waiter returns with our mimosas and we both order our lunch. Knowing we have a wedding coming up, we want to start dieting so we order salads. I get the spring salad with grilled chicken and fresh veggies and Maggie orders a chicken Caesar salad and a cup of soup. Look at us being all healthy.

"Yes, Ryan and I were talking last night and we decided we don't want to have a long engagement. So, we decided to get married in 2 months. So, that means the date is November 15th." Maggie starts clapping and bouncing up and down in her chair.

I am shocked. That is not like Maggie. "Oh wow, that's awesome. Well then, we better get to work then. Have you found a venue yet?"

"Yes, we wanted to get married at the Marina and then have the reception on a Yacht. I think it will be perfect. I already looked into it and it holds 115 guests, so that will also help with not having the wedding too big."

She is getting excited and I can't be happier for her. "Okay well that sounds great. After lunch let's walk over so you can show me and then maybe we can look at bridesmaid dresses."

We both eat our lunch in record time and Maggie pays the bill before I have a chance to argue with her. I'm not complaining of a free meal but she has a lot of stuff coming up that cost money.

As we walk toward the Marina, I see wildflowers on the side of the walkway and I can't stop thinking of the flowers again. I am sure it's nothing but it still feels weird. How did they get there if I didn't buzz anyone into the building? I guess they could have followed someone in, or someone else buzzed them in.

"Hey Maggie, when I was leaving to meet you earlier, I had flowers sitting outside my front door. The card read *I need you*. It seemed odd they were just left there. Do you think they could have been from Darren?"

Maggie looked puzzled, "I need you? If it was from Darren, it seems weird he would only write that on the card. Maybe they were delivered to the wrong place. Did it say who the florist was?"

"That was what I thought too. No, it was a blank card. It

looked like someone put it together themself, to be honest. I am sure it's nothing, it's just weird." I try to push it out of my mind and focus on my sister. We enter the Marina and walk directly to the event desk located in the lobby.

"Ah Maggie, it's nice to see you again. What can I do for you?" The event coordinator shakes my hand and hugs Maggie.

"Hi Ricardo, I wanted to show my sister the site where the ceremony and reception will be held, is that okay?" Maggie waves her hand around and Ricardo smiles.

"Yes, yes of course. Would you like me to take you, or do you feel comfortable walking around on your own?" Ricardo was being polite but you can tell he was busy. He had a stack of paperwork on his desk a foot high.

"Nope, I got this, I just wanted to make sure it was okay before I started walking around the Marina." Maggie motioned for me to follow her and off we went.

The ceremony location was beautiful. It was outside, on a deck and it overlooked the Marina. You could see all the boats floating by. This was perfect and it fit my sister and Ryan's personality well. After touring where the ceremony will be, she took me downstairs and we walked onto the yacht where the reception would be held. On the deck at the front would be cocktails, while the bridal party had their pictures done. Then at the back of the boat would have tables and chairs set up for dinner. There was also a section inside as well that had a bar, lounge area and bathrooms. This was perfect. It was also helpful to see it set up for another wedding. It gave you a better idea of how everything would look once the flowers and tables were arranged.

"Maggie, this is amazing and so perfect for you and Ryan." I give her a hug and we both start giggling. This is going to be an unforgettable wedding. I take a few quick pictures so I can show Darren when he returns home from his trip in a few days. I know he's going to think this place is just as awesome.

Over the next few hours Maggie has me try on about 15 different bridesmaid dresses. We were about to give up when I tried the last one hanging in the dressing room. The dress was a navy-blue strapless gown that crisscrossed in the back and the entire dress was sheer. It had a slit up the side but it was tasteful and elegant. The dress fit me perfectly and I wouldn't need anything done to it. There were tiny diamonds that bordered the front of the dress along the waistline. I loved this dress and I secretly hoped Maggie felt the same way. I stepped out of the dressing room and Maggie's eyes lit up.

She put her hands over her mouth, "Wow Tiffany you look gorgeous in that dress. It was like it was made for you. I think that is the dress for sure."

"Really? Because I like that green dress too. Are you sure?" I felt like I was holding my breath for her approval.

"Yes absolutely. Let's get it." Maggie stands up to try and get the sales lady's attention and I go back into the room to change. I am excited she liked this dress as much as I did. I feel sexy and beautiful and I can't wait to show Darren what it looks like. I have a feeling he will like it too. Maybe I should also buy some sexy lingerie to wear under the dress for afterward. I mean it is a wedding and all.

After I finish getting dressed, I set up an appt to come back in a month to try it on and make sure no alterations are needed. With me trying to eat better, hopefully, I can lose a few pounds.

Maggie insists on walking me back to my apartment so she can look at the flowers and card that mysteriously showed up at my apartment. I am glad she did too because as we approach my door there is an envelope taped to the front. On the envelope, it has my name handwritten in black ink. I look over at Maggie and I can tell she thinks this is just as weird as I do and probably somehow related to whoever left the flowers. On cue we both reach to grab the envelope. Maggie grabs it off the door and holds it away from me.

"Tiffany let's not just jump to any conclusions. Let's go inside and put down our stuff first, plus I could use a glass of wine." I nod in agreeance and let us both into my apartment.

Maggie puts her purse down on top of the envelope, "Hey, I am going to use your bathroom, I'll be back." Maggie walks down the hallway to the bathroom. I wait until I hear her before I grab the envelope. I stare at it for a few seconds before realizing I am wasting time and I rip it open before Maggie returns and tries to take it away from me. Inside is a plain white card that reads,

I will follow you to the end of the earth and back. You will always be mine, Tiffany.

- *XO*

Okay this is starting to get weird now. I need to show Maggie and Darren. What will Darren think? At first, with the flowers, I thought it could be Darren but now with the handwritten envelope, it couldn't be him since he is out of town. Who could this be if it isn't him and why? I haven't met anyone except Darren and Chase, since I moved here. I don't work with anyone, because I work from home, and the only people I hang out with is my family. I am almost positive this wasn't Chase. This was not his style, plus he is back with his ex-girlfriend.

Maggie walks into the kitchen and stops. She sees the ripped envelope in my hand and the look on my face. Even though this still could be Darren, my gut tells me otherwise. Something just feels off about this.

"Tiffany what is it? Let me see what it says."

I hand her the card and she read it at least 5 times before looking up at me. She doesn't say anything. She grabs her glass of wine, takes a sip and rereads the card for the 6th time. I grab my glass of wine and I sit down next to her. After a few minutes she grabs her phone and texts someone.

"Tiffany, you have no idea who could have sent you the flowers and card?" She raises her eyebrows and looks worried.

"No, I have no idea. Since I moved here you guys are the only ones who I have been hanging out with. I haven't even given anyone my new address. I am at a loss." I take a sip of my wine and close my eyes for a second. I need to clear my head. This is too weird. Like something from a movie where some guy stalks a girl... but we all know how that ends and I refuse to let myself continue thinking about it.

"Look I am sure it is nothing. It's probably Darren and we are getting all freaked out for nothing. Or it's probably some kid with a crush that I ran into at the store or something." I finish my glass of wine and pour another.

Maggie decides to stay with me until about 5 pm and then leaves for home. She and Ryan have a date to look at wedding invitations. Of course, Darren had to be out of town this week and isn't due to come home for another two days. I want to ask him about this but the last thing I want is to make him worry while he is out of town. After Maggie leaves, I lock the front door and make sure the sliding door to the balcony is locked too. It's weird. I lived in this apartment alone and I was fine, but now that Darren lives with me it feels different being alone.

I go back and forth for a while but eventually decide to call Darren and feel him out. I figure if I don't say anything and the flowers were from him, he would ask me if I got a delivery but it goes to voice mail.

"Hey babe, it's me. I just wanted to say I miss you and I can't wait to have you back home. Call me later if you can." I hang up the phone and get ready for the night.

I get myself another glass of wine and grab my laptop before crawling into bed and start working on my next article. I need to get my mind off from tonight. Something about today doesn't feel right and with all the weirdness, writing sounds like the perfect idea. There is nothing like a warm cozy bed, a nice glass of wine and my laptop to calm my nerves. It's just what I needed.

* * *

The next morning, I wake up to someone knocking on my front door. I must have fallen asleep in the middle of writing. I still have my laptop open and I didn't even finish my wine. I grab my robe and run my hands through my hair as I move toward the door.

I open the door and freeze. I cannot move let alone speak to the person standing in front of me. It's like I am paralyzed. I can scream and yell at myself to move, but my body won't listen. Why won't my body listen to me to go run away? The person standing in front of me is like a ghost and the sight before my eyes is a bad dream. After a few seconds, I shake my head and take a step back into my apartment. No this cannot be happening. What is he doing here? How did he even find me? The one person I never expected to see again is standing right in front of me. And he is smiling with eyes that are cold and sharp like ice.

"Todd... what are you doing here?" I start to stumble over my words. I blink and blink again to make sure the person that is standing in front of me is in fact him. And it is. As much as I want this to be a horrible dream, I know I am not that lucky. It's real, and I am frightened.

"Hey baby, did you miss me? I sure missed you." He starts to walk forward and I realize I have the door wide open. I lunge forward and try to shut the door but he blocks it with his foot and keeps pushing his way in. He's strong and it doesn't take much for him to overpower me.

"Todd, stop! Get out of my apartment. I don't have anything to say to you." I keep trying to push him away and close the door but it is no use. Todd makes his way into the apartment and closes the door. I turn and back away but he is too fast and moves closer, closing the gap I am desperately trying to make between us. We lock eyes and I don't think I have ever been this scared in my life.

Todd glances down my body and back up to my eyes, and

smiles, "Damn you are sexy baby. I missed you."

He walks closer and reaches for my hand, but I swat it away and try to run. He grabs my side and holds on to me. My back is now against his chest and I can feel him breathing on my neck. I feel his disgusting hot breath blowing on my neck and I close my eyes and try not to cry.

"Don't tease me Tiffany. You are barely wearing anything right now. I know you want to feel my hands touch you. It's been too long." Todd starts to kiss my neck and he moves his hand down my side and around my waste.

Todd is starting to lift my nightshirt and I try to move but he has a tight grip on my other arm. I keep trying to move away but that only makes him grip my arm tighter.

"Please Todd. Stop. I don't want this. What are you doing here? You shouldn't be here." I start to cry and I don't know what to do. He is overpowering me and I can't stop him. I can feel his fingers starting to move down the front of me and all I can think about is getting away before this ends badly. He was aggressive towards the end of our relationship, but he never would have taken it this far.

"You know you miss feeling me baby. We need to start over and make this work. I fucked up before but I can make it up to you. I can make you feel good again." Todd starts groping my breasts and I can feel how aroused he is and I am disgusted. I can smell the liquor on his breath and it makes my stomach curl. He had trouble in college managing his drinking, but I was always there to help him balance it. I guess after I left him, he started drinking again.

All I want to do his wake up from this bad dream but reality is playing an evil trick on me. I start to cry harder, scream and try to get out of his hold, but nothing works. My heart is beating and it's so loud I can't think straight.

"Todd please stop touching me. You are hurting me. I don't want you. I am seeing someone else now. Please get off me." Soon as the words leave my mouth, I knew it was the wrong thing to say. Telling Todd that I am seeing someone was a big mistake. I force my eyes open and try and calm down. I know that this is the only way if I want to try and escape his hold.

Todd turns me around so we are facing each other, "What are you trying to do to me Tiffany, hurt me? We are engaged and you are with someone else?"

Todd looks pissed and not himself. I don't recognize the person staring back at me. His eyes don't look the same. Like it's a different person staring at me. What is wrong with him?

Todd shakes his head to regain focus and I find an opportunity to break away and put some distance between us.

"Yes, I am seeing someone else. I left you Todd. You cheated on me with Julie. Our engagement has been over now for over 7 months now. What did you expect?" I am so confused. What the hell is going on?

Todd looks like he is going to explode with rage. He's had a temper in the past but I have never been scared for my life before now. He lets me go and starts pacing back and forth. Every few seconds he pounds on his chest with his fist and I know that's my opportunity to try to get away from him. I slowly start to back up and notice my cell phone sitting on the coffee table. I just need to make it there and grab it. Little by little I inch my way closer and closer to the table.

I start to reach for the cell phone and I can see the front door opening. My heart starts racing. Maybe someone finally heard me screaming and they came to help me. Todd stops pacing and starts to walk over to me. He hasn't realized someone is starting to open the front door. I don't move because my eyes are fixed on the person who is walking in. Just as Todd grabs me and kisses me, Darren walks through and stops dead in his tracks.

I can only imagine how this must look to him. I am barely wearing any clothes, and a man is holding me, trying to kiss me. Darren stands there staring at me. He doesn't move, he doesn't speak, he looks broken.

"Darren!!! Wait, this isn't what it looks like. Please, Todd let me go. You are such an asshole." I break free from Todd's grip and I rush to the door toward Darren where he is standing now looking at Todd.

Todd starts to laugh and holds up his hands, "Hey man sorry, she didn't tell me she was with anyone."

Darren looks back down at me and shakes his head. He starts to back away and walks out the door. He doesn't say anything, he just leaves.

I rush down the stairs after him but he is too quick. I scream his name but nothing stops him. Darren jumps in his truck and leaves. Tears are running down my face making it hard to see anything. I try to wipe them away but it's no use, they won't stop.

How did I go from everything being perfect to everything being completely fucked up within 10 minutes? I am standing barefoot on the sidewalk. I am barely dressed and cars are driving by. People are staring at me and I don't care. All I care about is Darren and what he must be thinking. I feel a hand on my shoulder and lookup. It's Todd.

"Hey beautiful, till next time." Todd turns and walks to his car parked out front.

What an asshole. Why does he keep trying to ruin my life? I need to put an end to this. I thought I already had since I left him and drove across the country but I guess that wasn't enough. And now he shows up, forces himself on me at the exact moment Darren walks through the door. This couldn't have been staged any better.

I run back up to my apartment and lock the door. I grab my cellphone and collapse in my bed. I can't believe this is happening. I try Darren's cell but it goes straight to voice mail. I keep calling but I know he turned off his phone. I cry for I don't know how long, but at some point, I must have passed out. I awake to my sister sitting on the side of my bed, stroking my hair, and telling me that everything will be okay. I start to cry again and this time, I have no more tears to shed. I feel defeated and ruined. I feel like I hit rock bottom and there is no way I can come back from this. This is one fucked up situation and this isn't even my fault this time. Not only did Todd find me and abuse me, but Darren thinks I cheated on him. Where do I even go from here?

CHAPTER THIRTEEN

Over the next few days I stay in bed and cry. I called Darren about a hundred times and he never answers. He is refusing to speak to me and let me explain. Even Maggie and Ryan tried to tell him but he wouldn't listen. Soon as either of them starts to talk about it, Darren would either walk away or hang up on them. I know how it must have looked but I didn't do anything wrong and now I am starting to get angry for how he is treating me.

My phone starts to ring and I jump. Lately everything startles me. From car horns, alarms to pretty much any loud noise, and all that is thanks to Todd. I get out of bed to answer it. The phone is laying on the floor across the room. I am lucky it still works. After I got fed up from Darren not answering my calls, I threw it last night. One of those moments I regretted soon as the phone left my hand.

"Oh hello." It's Maggie on the other line and I know I sound disappointed but I really thought it might be Darren.

"Hey Tiffany, get dressed. I'll be at your apartment in 20

mins to pick you up. Where something cute." The phone goes dead.

What the hell was that? I take a quick shower and blow dry my hair. By the time I start my makeup I hear Maggie letting herself in my apartment.

"Tiffany you better be almost ready!" Maggie walks into my bedroom and looks relieved.

I look at Maggie through my mirror while I finish my makeup, "Why do I have to wear something cute? Where are we going?"

Maggie smiles, "I thought we can have brunch today. You need to get out of the house, plus I found a nice place that has bottomless mimosas." Okay now she is talking my language.

I raise my eyebrows slightly. I can use a drink for sure, and the way I am feeling, bottomless mimosas sound perfect. I choose a sundress and flat sandals. I just bought the dress a few weeks ago but haven't had a chance to wear it yet. It's a form-fitting dress with spaghetti straps. It comes a few inches above the knee which makes it sexy but still appropriate to wear out. It's white with blue flowers and it zips in the back. I love the dress and it fits me perfectly.

Maggie drives since I have no idea where we are going and after about 15 minutes of silence we finally arrive. It's a cute little restaurant on the water. I am glad Maggie dragged me out of the house. I need to stop letting men ruin my life. I cried too many times over how men treat me and I am done. We give our name to the hostess and she shows us to our table. The restaurant is beautiful and we can see the water and boats as they all sail by.

"So, Tiffany, have you heard from Todd at all since the

other day?" She takes a sip of her water and I can tell she is hoping I don't start crying.

"No, it's weird. He hasn't tried coming by or tried to call. Don't get me wrong, I am relieved. I don't want to see him again but why show up and then disappear?"

"Who knows Tiffany, but if he comes by again, call the cops. I still think you should put a restraining order in." Maggie looks serious and I know I need to tell her.

"I did actually. I called yesterday and you know what? He has another one out from someone else too." The waitress comes over and we tell her we would like the bottomless mimosas and some bread to start.

Maggie looks concerned after the waitress leaves. "How scary is that? Look I don't want you staying alone. Why don't you stay with me and Ryan until we figure everything out?"

"Look Maggie, I appreciate that but I will be fine. Really! You don't need to worry about me." I smile, and hope she buys what I am selling. I do not want to bother Maggie and Ryan. They should be alone and enjoying their engagement, not having me tag along and be the annoying houseguest that doesn't leave.

The drinks and bread arrive and the waitress tells us she will be right back to take our order. Everything on the menu looks awesome but since Darren left, I haven't had much of an appetite. I lost 5 pounds over this fight. I look up from my menu to see if Maggie is ready to order, and she has this guilty look on her face. Just as I am about to ask her what's wrong, I hear the hostess behind me say, *and here is your table with the rest of your party. Enjoy gentlemen.*

I look up and freeze. Ryan and Darren are both standing there staring at me and Maggie. I knew it was too good to be true. Maggie just couldn't leave it alone. Of course, she had to stick her sisterly nose in my business.

"What the hell is he doing here Maggie?" I stand up and go to grab my purse.

Ryan puts his hand out to stop me from leaving, "Wait Tiffany, we just wanted to get you and Darren together so you can talk. That's all."

Darren looks just as pissed as I do, "I told you both to stay out of this. It is none of your business and I don't want to see her."

My head snaps up. Wait, did he just say what I think he said? "Hold on, I'm sorry, did you say you don't want to see me? Well the feeling is mutual buddy. I don't know who you think you are but you need a reality check. I didn't do anything wrong! You walked out on me when I needed you more than ever."

Darren starts to laugh, "You didn't do anything wrong? You are ridiculous you know that? I go out of town and the first thing you do is sleep with someone else. You would have thought that since you know what it was like to be cheated on you wouldn't do that. I can see I was wrong."

I am shocked he just said that. I can't speak. Tears start filling up and now I can barely see.

Ryan pushed Darren a little to get his attention, "What the hell man. If you would listen to us you would know she didn't cheat on you. That asshole was Todd and he tried to force himself on her."

I can't stand here anymore, I grab my purse and run out of

the restaurant as fast as I can. I pass the waitress on my way out and she looks confused. Lucky for me there was a couple getting out of a cab and soon as they exit, I jump in and ask the driver if he can take me home. I hope Darren feels like shit. Why couldn't he give me the benefit of the doubt? How could he possibly think I would cheat on him? I have so many unanswered questions, but right now all I can think about is getting as far away from him as I can. Far from everyone to be honest. I can't believe they would pull something like this knowing how I felt about Darren and how he feels about me.

I know everyone will be following me back to my apartment to make sure I'm okay so when I arrive, I quickly pay the cab driver, race up the stairs and pack a bag along with my computer. I have no idea where I am going, but I know I need to get far away from here. I start pulling clothes off the hangers and shoving my shoes into my bag. I am completely packed and in my car within 15 minutes.

I start the car, turn the music up, and turn my phone off before they start to call and I change my mind. The only thing that I am thinking about now is where to go. I put the car into drive and head out of town without looking back, without crying, without fear or any care for leaving them behind. I need some me time and this is exactly what I am going to do. I am not running; I am leaving the heartache and disappointment behind. Moving forward...

* * *

"What do you mean she is gone? Where the hell did she go, Maggie?" Darren runs his hands through his hair and sits on the couch.

Maggie starts to yell, "I have no idea Darren, but I do know she left because there are a bunch of hangers-on the floor, her dresser drawers are open and her hair and makeup stuff are gone. Not to mention her computer. Maybe if you didn't yell at her in the restaurant in front of everyone, we wouldn't be standing in her apartment without her."

"I'm sorry okay? I had no idea that guy was Todd and I just lost it. I know I acted like a jealous idiot, but you have no idea how much she means to me. Hell, it's only been a few months since we met, but I already want to marry her." Darren starts pacing back and forth and running his hands in his hair.

Ryan tries to turn the situation around, "Okay so we know she turned her phone off but she has to turn it back on at some point. We just need to wait until she does it."

Darren stops, "I can't wait that long. It could be days Ryan. I just want to talk to her and let her know how sorry I am."

Ryan shakes his head, "I know you don't want to hear this right now but you don't have a choice. Let her cool off and think. You owe her that at least. She just needs some time to think and process everything."

"Fine, alright. I know you are right. I'll give her some space." Darren grabs his keys off the table and leaves the apartment.

* * *

I jump on I-95 south and just drive. I have no idea where I'm going. I kind of like the idea of not knowing where I'll end up.

It's kind of thrilling and exciting, and not like me at all. I know wherever I end up though, I will have to call Maggie at some point. She will worry and then tell my parents and I can't have them worrying about me too.

3 hours have passed and I realize how close to Savannah I am. I have always wanted to go back since my girls' trip in college. I guess I am going back now. I get off the exit and turn on my phone to get directions to a hotel. Soon and my phone charges up, I have 12 missed calls and 4 voice mails. I'll deal with that later. Now it's direction time.

"Siri, find a hotel in Savannah." Siri finds me a nice hotel and it has a spa on site. Perfect! I call the hotel and they have some rooms available. Normally I can't eat by myself let alone go on a trip, but something is different this time around. I have all this courage and energy. I press on the gas and continue heading toward Savannah.

I arrive at the hotel and the valet takes my car and bags for me. 10 minutes later I'm in my room and I have a view of the city overlooking the water. It's beautiful and peaceful and I can watch the people down below walk around. Some are couples, some are locals sitting and painting and others are street vendors trying to make a dollar selling handmade crafts to tourists. I remember I have a crap load of missed calls and voice mails. I know I need to face them sooner or later but I think I need some wine for this. I grab my phone and wallet and head to the lobby bar. It's nice. The wall behind the bar is a fish tank. They have live music playing and it's not too busy yet. I grab a seat at the bar and order a glass of wine before I start to listen to my voice mails.

The first voice mail is from Maggie.

Hey Tiffany. That was not how I wanted this to go. Please know Ryan and I only wanted to help. Please call me back.

The second voice mail is from Darren.

I am so, so, sorry babe. Please call me back. I had no idea that was Todd. I owe you a huge apology and I want to do it in person. I love you.

My heart breaks a little when I hear him tell me he loves me. I love him so much, but he hurt me. How can he not trust me after everything we have been through? The first thought he had was that I cheated on him. He didn't even give me a chance to explain what he walked into.

The third and fourth voice mail was Darren again.

Baby please answer the phone. Where are you? Just tell me and I will come to you. We can get past this. I know I fucked up.

Damn it Peaches. Please call me. I can't stand not knowing if you are okay.

I erase the voice mails and then I send a quick text to my sister so she doesn't worry. Even though she didn't leave me an abundance of voice mails, the majority of my missed calls were from her. I start to send her a text and I erase it. I type out another message and erase that one too. Ugh, I don't know what to say without sounding rude. I know she did what she did to help me, but I cannot get past this. She and Ryan were wrong and she needs to stop interfering in my life.

Maggie, I am okay. Please do not worry about me. I need some time to be alone. I feel ambushed and confused. I need time to think about everything. I know that you and Ryan meant no harm and I am not mad at you guys. I am mad at the situation and for Darren not giving me the benefit of the doubt. When I am ready to talk, I will reach back out again. Love ya, XOXOXOX

I hit send before I can delete it and put my phone back in my purse. Okay, now that's been dealt with, time to relax. I take a sip of my wine and look around the bar. A few couples are talking and having dinner together. There are a few individuals by themself, glued to their phone, and a small group of women, who look to be out on a girl's night. And then there is me. A sad lonely girl at the bar, drinking alone, trying to figure out where her life went wrong.

I order another glass of wine from the bartender. He is cute, kind of young, but cute. There are not many people sitting at the bar. Most of them are sitting at the tables in the lounge area where the live music is.

"Here you look like you can use this, it's on me." The bartender smiles and gives me a wink before he walks away to help another customer.

I stare at the shot. It's clear and it has salt on the rim with lime. I know right away it's Tequila. Don't get me wrong, I like Tequila, but I haven't had it in a while. I pick up the shot and shoot it. It chilled so that makes it a little easier to go down. I shake a little from the after taste. It's smoother than most Tequilas and you can tell it's not cheap.

I wave the bartender over, "Excuse me. Thanks for the shot.

What type of Tequila was that? It was really smooth." I smile and put the lime into the shot glass, pushing it forward.

"Ah this was Clase Azul Respado Tequila. I'm glad you liked it." He shows me the bottle and then pours two shots, pushing one forward toward me. "Here is to letting go of whatever has you upset, it's not worth stressing over."

We both shoot back the shot and start laughing. "Thanks, I needed this to help relax a little and forget why I came here." I smile, and then realize I am staring at him so I glance away.

"So, what's your name? I'm Aaron." He reaches over the bar and shakes my hand.

"My name is Tiffany, it's nice to meet you, Aaron." I bite my bottom lip to stop from smiling again, but that only draws his attention. I can see his eyes travel down to my lips and my heart starts racing. What the hell am I doing? I did not come here for this. Don't get me wrong, Aaron is extremely good looking. I can tell he has a good body. He has that rugged look to him but is still well-groomed at the same time.

Aaron walks back over to me after helping a few customers and leans forward so he is closer to me. He puts down a bottle of Tequila, two shot glasses and a plate of limes on the bar top. He also has a small plate of chips and salsa. "Here I thought we could use another drink and here is a snack to help soak up the liquor." Aaron gives me a little wink.

Oh my God this guy is sexy. "Thanks, Aaron, that was nice of you. I grab the bottle and pour the Tequila into the two shot glasses. Aaron raises his eyebrows and smiles. "Okay Aaron, here is to stop letting people run your life." I shoot the shot back but Aaron stands there staring at me. He doesn't drink his.

"So, who has you all pissed? Clearly a sexy woman like yourself doesn't come sit at a bar alone, drink Tequila and keeps a bartender company for no reason." Aaron takes his shot and smiles. He leans forward so I can only I can hear him, "Whatever it is, ask yourself if it is worth getting this upset over. And if you need help getting back at anyone, I would be happy to help you." Aaron puts his empty shot glass on the counter, winks and walks away.

Wow! How can this be happening right now? There is this sexy ass guy clearly hitting on me. At any point I can give in and let him make me feel better. I want to feel better! What is it with me and guys at bars? I want to stop hurting, I want to give in to the temptation but I can't. It will only make the situation worse. I can already tell I have a buzz. I need to eat something quick before I make a bad decision. I grab a few chips and dip them in the salsa. A few minutes later the chips are gone, and I start to feel the Tequila now.

I am so sick of men treating me like crap. I gulp the rest of my wine and reach into my purse for my phone. Before I know it, I call Darren and he picks up on the first ring which catches me off guard a little.

"Hello, Tiffany, thank God you are okay. Where are you?" Darren sounds worried.

"Stop calling me Darren. That's it! I can't handle you. Well, I mean I can handle you, but you keep making my phone thing ring off the hook." My words are starting to slur slightly. You can tell I am a little drunk.

"Tiffany, you are drunk. Where are you baby so I can come

and get you?" Darren pleads for me to tell him where I am.

"Nope, no sir-ee. You will not know where I am. I am relaxing at a nice hotel, and the bar has a fish tank. Did you know that?" I start to lose track of why I called and I grab my wine, forgetting it is empty.

"Hey Aaron, another glass of wine sweetie." I smile, and then realize I still have Darren on the phone.

"Tiffany who the hell is Aaron? Where are you? I am not comfortable with you being alone in this state of mind." Darren is trying to keep calm but I can tell he is about to lose his shit. I need to end the call soon.

"It's none of your concern Darren. Maybe if you didn't walk out on me, and yell at me, you would be in Savan..., here with me right now. I got to go." I end the call and grab my glass of wine.

After another 15 minutes I charge everything to my room, thank Aaron for keeping me company and I leave. Luckily the elevators are close and my room is only on the 3rd floor so I don't have a far walk. I hate being this drunk, but it was necessary tonight.

Before I make it to my hotel door, I am taking off my shoes. My feet hurt and I feel like I am suffocating in my clothes. Soon as the door to my room shuts, I rip off my dress and climb into bed naked. Of course, I would have to be here naked, in an awesome town, with no boyfriend. This is my life! I hate being this way. I bet Darren is already sleeping and not worrying about anything.

I reach for my phone and start to smile. I know exactly what to do. I pull the sheet up just above my breasts but leave my leg out. I flip my hair over and lean back slightly so my boobs push out. I grab my phone and take a selfie. I look hot and before I chicken out, I send Darren the picture and type, **this is what you are missing**.

I don't wait for a response. I put my phone on silent and turn the light out. Today has been exhausting and I don't want to deal with it anymore. I want to forget everything that happened today. Hopefully tomorrow will be the start of something new. No more drama, no more guy issues. Just a new start. I start to plan out tomorrow in my head as I drift off to sleep. I want to take a ferry and maybe check out the restaurant on the roof. I don't get far in planning out my day before I fall asleep.

CHAPTER FOURTEEN

The next day I awake to someone pounding on my door. I must have been exhausted because I slept until 10 am. Dang, I never sleep this late. I get up and grab the complimentary robe from the bathroom before yelling to whoever is banging that I will be just a moment. I look through the peephole and I am shocked. I look through it again, yup, it's Darren on the other side of the door. How the hell did he find me?

I open the door and he is standing there alone with a duffle bag and his phone in the other hand.

Darren stares right at me. He looks relieved and pissed at the same time. "She finally answered the door, Maggie. I'll call you later."

My mouth drops and I don't believe what's going on. I told Maggie I needed some time to myself, and she helps Darren track me down? See if she gets any more wedding help from me.

"What are you doing here Darren, and how in the hell did

you even find me?" I stand in the doorway, not budging. I cannot give in this time.

"Well, when you send me a half-naked picture, next time make sure the hotel key on your nightstand is not in the picture. I got the name from your room key. Besides I grew up around here, remember?" He starts laughing a little and put's his phone in his pocket.

"Darren you need to go back home. I don't want to see you, and you are not staying with me. As you can see, I am fine." I start to close my door and he stops me.

"Look, I know I fucked up. I will spend the rest of my life making that up to you. I never want you to feel like I do not trust you. I just freaked out. This is new to me too Tiffany. But I do know that I don't want to lose you." Darren looks exhausted like he hasn't slept all night.

"Darren, I need time. I don't know if I can be with someone who doesn't trust me. And I don't trust that how you acted won't happen again. You broke me. Don't you get that? Now I need to go. Sorry, you drove all the way here for nothing." I close the door but I don't move. I am going against everything not to open the door and leap in his arms.

"I didn't come here for nothing Tiffany. I came here for you." Darren picks up his bag and walks back down the hallway toward the elevators.

I can't believe that was it. Is he really giving up that easy? I try to shake off my morning interruption and get myself dressed. I know the hotel has a great brunch menu and I am starving. After I get dressed, I head down to the lobby restaurant to get something to eat before I start my day of sightseeing. I grab a seat at the bar and order a mimosa while I look over the menu.

I can feel the presence of someone walking up next to me, and they lean on the bar to get my attention. I know it has to be Darren but I refuse to look up.

"Do you mind if I sit here." The voice sounds familiar but tired. He pulls out the chair and sits before I can respond.

"Darren, I thought you left?" I must look surprised because he smiles at me and then touches my shoulder.

"I told you, I did not come here for nothing. I came here for you Peaches and if I have to stay here because you won't leave, then I am staying here." Darren turns away toward the bartender. "Excuse me, can I get a mimosa and a menu please?"

"Fine, stay Darren. Whatever." I try not to smile but deep down there is a part of me that is excited. Darren ran after me. Todd didn't do that when I left. He didn't even call me. Darren is fighting for us, and I need to give him that at least.

We both order our breakfast and get another round of drinks. We don't speak to each other much. I am grateful he is giving me a chance to assess the situation and figure out how I want to deal with this. After we finish breakfast, Darren asks the bartender to charge both of our breakfasts to his room. Wait, what? Did he book a hotel room here?

That got my attention. My head shot up. I was shocked. "Darren, you are staying here in Savannah, at this hotel?"

"Yes, I told you I am not leaving. When are you going to believe what I am telling you?" He takes ahold of my hand and stands up for me to follow him. "Please let's take a walk and we can talk about everything. Or not talk. I just want to be with you."

I let out a smile. I can't help it. He is being really sweet, and if he is trying this hard, then maybe I will see what happens. I take his hand and we leave the hotel and head out into the city. I have no idea where we are going. We just start walking in silence. It's nice. We walk for a few blocks and we end up at the water. I can see giant boats going by and it reminds me of home. I lean against the railing and take a deep breath. I can feel Darren's eyes on me.

I stare out into the water, too afraid to look at Darren. "I love you so much. Sometimes it scares me how much I love you because I know if anything goes wrong, it will be excruciating and I don't know if I can handle it."

Darren stays quiet and I am thankful he is letting me talk. "Every time I close my eyes, I see your face. That look you had when you came home and saw me and Todd. That look on your face broke my heart. I don't know how you could have thought so little of me to assume I cheated on you while you were away." Tears start to roll down my cheek.

Darren touches my cheek and slowly wipes away my tears. "Tiffany, I love you too. More than anything in this world. The way you make me feel, I can't even explain. I know I handled this all wrong. Love makes you do crazy things, I guess. I used to think that was bullshit but now I get it. I promise you that I will never make you feel like this again."

I turn and face Darren. I know deep down that he loves me and is sorry. I want nothing more to feel his arms wrapped around me and his lips on my lips. I lean forward and hug Darren, laying my head on his chest. I don't say a word. I just stand there and let him wrap his arms around me. I feel him take a huge breath of relief and the tension in his body language disappears.

"Baby, do you want to keep walking around, or can I take you back to the hotel?" I can feel his heart beating fast as if he is almost scared to hear of my response.

I glance up and give Darren a soft kiss on the lips. "Please take my back to the hotel."

We walk the few blocks hand and hand back to the hotel and with each step I feel the tension washing away and the nervousness in my stomach building. I can't wait to be alone with him. I need to feel him more than anything right now.

We step into the elevator and Darren pushes the button for the third floor. Soon as the doors close, he picks me up and pushes my back toward the elevator wall. Immediately I wrap my legs around his waist. Darren starts kissing my neck while he moves his hands under my dress. I can feel his hands grab my ass and start squeezing me. He's rough, but it's exactly what we both need. The elevator chimed and the doors open. Neither of us cares. He starts to walk out of the elevator and to my door without putting me down. Even if I would have tried to get down, I don't think he would have let me.

We make it to my room and I press my room key on the keypad to open the door. Darren pushes it open and lets the weight of the door slam shut. He moves right to the bed and within seconds he is removing my clothes and I am taking off his pants. We don't talk. We just move with each other. Somehow, we both know exactly what each other needs. I can't get enough of his lips and hands on me. Darren lays on top of me and pins my hands above my head. He starts to kiss my lips and then moves down toward my neck. He feels amazing and I know I don't want this to end.

I spread my legs giving him easier access and immediately I can feel him start to slide into me. We have been together many times before, but something feels different. I can tell he wants the control and I let him have it. Darren's breathing is getting quicker and I can feel him move faster and faster. I match his rhythm and I hear him moan when he takes breaks from kissing my neck.

I'm panting and I barely can get out any words. "Darren, I needed this so much."

He leans forward and I start to scream with relief and I let go. My orgasm is so intense. Darren moves his arms from mine, placing them under my back giving him a better angle. Our eyes lock, and I bite my bottom lip and continue to stare at him, "Kiss me Darren."

We both lay there for an hour before either of us start to move. I don't want him to go. I don't want this to end. Darren starts to get up and I reach out and grab his arm.

He takes my hand off his arm and kisses it, "I'll be right back. I just need to use the bathroom and then I thought we could order some room service. I don't plan on leaving this bed, but we need to refuel."

I smile and sit up in the bed. While he is in the bathroom, I start to look at the room service menu. I am starving and can eat just about anything. I hear the bathroom door open and I look up. Darren is so sexy and I just lost all track of thought.

Darren walks back to bed naked, and I don't want food anymore. The only thing I want now is him. I start to move toward him as he gets under the covers and he starts laughing. "Hold on baby, we need to eat before we have another round, or two." He winks at me and the fire between my legs aches even more. I know he is right though. I am hungry, plus over the last week I lost some weight from all the stress.

"Fine, fine, fine. Here is the menu. I think I want a pizza and a salad." I hand him the menu and while he looks over it, I kiss his neck, with little kisses down to his collarbone where I start to make little circles with my tongue.

Darren finally gives up and tosses the menu on the floor. He flips me over on my stomach and kisses the side of my neck. Being with him feels amazing.

After round two, we finally order our food. We share a pizza and we even order a nice bottle of wine. I can't believe how this trip turned out. It went from me running away to be alone, to a trip where we don't leave the bed. I am glad it turned out this way though. I am laying between Darren's legs with my back pressed against his chest. He is rubbing my arm and I am so relaxed and happy. I don't want to get back to reality and face what is waiting for us at home.

I feel Darren take a huge breath, "Baby, I don't want to ruin this moment, but we do need to talk about everything. Maggie and Ryan told me some stuff, but I want us to talk about it. I need you to tell me exactly what happened."

I knew this conversation was coming, I just didn't think it was going to happen yet. "I know. I am just so scared. I am afraid of what you will think or do. Please just let me finish before you interrupt me. I want the chance to tell you everything."

Darren takes a sip of wine, "I promise. Turn around so I can see you Peaches."

I'm scared and nervous. What if he leaves again? I don't think I could handle it. I turn around so we are both facing each other and I take a deep breath. Here goes nothing.

"I woke up to someone knocking on our apartment door. I was tired and I didn't even think to look through the peephole before answering the door. It was Todd. Immediately I tried to shut the door but he barged through it. When I tried to run, he grabbed me and pinned me between him and the back of the couch. He kept telling me that he was back, that he missed me and wanted to be with me. I started crying and told him to let me go. I told Todd I was with someone and I didn't want to be with him. That was when he started to get angry. I could smell the liquor on his breath and in the past when he was like this, he used to get violent. I was so scared he was going to hurt me."

Tears start to run down my face, and I wipe them away with my hand.

"Todd moved his hands between my legs and started groping me. The more I struggled to get away, the rougher he became. I don't know how but somehow, I managed to break free and move across the room to get away. That's was when you walked in. I promise Darren, what happened was not something I wanted. He forced it. Please don't hate me."

Tears continue to roll down my face, and Darren just sits there in shock. I don't think he knows what to say. I can't read him.

"Darren, please say something. Anything." I plead for him to acknowledge what I just told him. Finally, he speaks but his voice sounds different.

"I am so sorry baby. I can't believe what that bastard did to you, and here I go and treat you like that. I am no better than he is." Darren looks at me with remorse and defeat.

"No Darren, please, you had no idea what he did. I understand that now. I don't want this to stand between us anymore. Let's move on. I need you more than anything right now." I reach forward and Darren hugs me.

"I will never again walk away and not be there for you." Darren starts to rub my back. I switch positions so I can lay down with him. He holds me in his arms and he continues to rub my back until eventually, we both drift asleep.

CHAPTER FIFTEEN

Darren looks so peaceful, not to mention so damn sexy sleeping in my bed. I can't sleep, and I know if I continue to toss and turn it will wake him up. I quietly slip out and head to the bathroom. I don't recognize the person staring back at me in the mirror. I came to Savannah to get away, clear my head, and think about what I should do next. I wasn't even alone 24 hours and I am already back in bed with the guy who was the reason I fled from home in the first place. I splash cold water on my face and try to snap out of it. I can't keep being wishy-washy as my mother would call it. I need to own my actions and stop questioning if what I am doing is right. Am I happy? Yes... Would I be happier if Darren was not in my life? Heck no! This is my answer.

I finish washing my face and clean myself up a little before heading back into the room. Darren and I need to talk but before I move on, there's something I have to do first. I am glad he came after me, but he hurt me. I open the bathroom door just a crack and

I can see he is still sleeping. I reach into my bag to find something to wear and try my best to get dressed without making too much noise. I finish packing all my clothes and personal items I had scattered around and do one last sweep of the room before he wakes up. It's not that I don't want to make this work. I do, but I need to clear my head and process last night on my own. Without the influence of Darren. I use the next few minutes to write him a note before I sneak out of the hotel room.

Darren,

I just need more time. Please understand that. Thanks for listening last night...

-Always yours,
Tiffany

I gently place the note on my pillow, and slowly back away and out of the hotel room. Luckily, it's still early in the morning, so not many people are up. The elevator doors open immediately and I take a quick breath before stepping into the elevator. My heart is racing and I start to get scared. He can wake up any minute, see the note, and come chasing after me. When the doors open to the lobby, I grab my bag and practically run toward the door that leads outside.

"May I have your valet ticket please?" The Valet attended has his hand reached out and looks annoyed I wasn't prepared. I don't know why since I am the only one here.

"Umm, just a second, I am sorry." I frantically start digging through my purse until I find it and I give it to the valet attendant.

He smiles and assures me it will only be a few moments. While I am waiting for him to return with my car, I grab a few dollars so I can tip him. I always feel weird if I don't, even if it says tipping not necessary on the sign outside.

My car pulls up and the attendant places my bag in the trunk for me. "Thank you, I appreciate the help." I quickly hand him the money and turn to get in my car and that's when I hear Darren. He is yelling and running across the lobby toward me. For a split second we lock eyes. I shake my head, and mouth sorry. I can't face him yet. I need to be on my own and think about what I want. How I am going to handle Darren and Todd and what I want my future to look like. I am tired of everyone telling me what I want or what I should do.

I shut my door and put the car in drive at the same time Darren makes it to my car and starts banging on the window.

"Tiffany, please don't do this. Stop the car." Darren is only wearing a pair of shorts. He doesn't even have shoes on. He must have read my note and put the first thing on he could find before exiting the hotel room.

Tears are starting to run down my face. I don't look at him through my driver's window, I stay looking straight and slowly start to drive forward. I can hear Darren yelling but I cannot make out what he is saying anymore. I just keep driving until the banging stops. When I look out my rearview mirror, all I see is a man standing there looking helpless and confused. Darren throws his hands up in the air but doesn't move. He continues to look at my car until I am out of sight and we cannot see each other anymore.

* * *

I merge onto the highway and just drive. I don't even realize I am heading home, not until I see the sign that says Welcome to North Carolina anyways. I need to face everyone eventually but there is something I need to do first. I decided to call my sister even though I am still annoyed with her. We need to talk and I know she is the one person that will understand me and not judge. I pick up the phone and select her name from the recent calls list on my screen and she answers on the first ring.

"Hey Maggie, I am almost home, can you meet me at my apartment alone so we can talk?" She agrees to meet me in 20 minutes and says she will bring over something for us to eat. I pull up to my apartment and just as I am grabbing my bags, I see Maggie walking toward me.

"Thank God you are okay. You had all of us so worried about you." Maggie gives me a lighthearted smile and a hug. "Tiffany please don't do that again."

I hug her back, "Let's go inside. It looks like it is about to rain."

Maggie and I get comfortable on the couch and I start telling her everything that happened while she pours us some wine. She doesn't say a word, which I am thankful for. She nods a few times and looks shocked but doesn't say anything. After about 10 minutes of talking non-stop, I catch my breath.

Maggie smiles a guilty half-smile and puts her hand on my arm. "You have to know what I did, I was only trying to help. I

163

know you and Darren love each other and Ryan and I just wanted to try and get you both together so you can talk it through. I never meant for you to think I was going behind your back."

I hold up my hand, "I know Mags. I know. I am not mad at you guys, just annoyed at the entire situation, but now I have no idea what to do. Darren followed me to Savannah, we made up a few times and then the next morning I freaked out and took off. I swear Maggie, you should have seen his face when I drove off." Tears start to fill my eyes and I blink to try and hold back from crying. Why do I keep going back and forth? One minute I want this to work out and the next I feel like it's over.

"Tiffany, do you love Darren? If you do, you need to stop running and face this head-on. To be honest, I think you need to face Todd too or you will never be able to continue what you and Darren were building." Maggie takes a sip of her wine and stares at me, waiting for my response.

I know Maggie is right and honestly that is the reason I left Savannah and came home. I feel like a chicken. I am so afraid to see Todd again, but I know I need closure.

It's like Maggie is reading my mind. She stands up, grabs my phone out of my purse and hands it to me. "Tiffany, call Todd. Ask him to meet you somewhere in public to talk. I will come with you in case he tries anything. This needs to end now." Her hands are crossed over her chest and I know I don't have a choice. I know I need to see him and end this once in for all. I need to put the past behind me if I want to move on and officially be with Darren.

I dial Todd's number he and answers right away. I tell Todd we need to talk and ask him to meet me at the restaurant down the street. I am surprised he agreed and it makes me even more uncomfortable. It's not like him to agree and listen to me without pushing back or making some nasty comment.

Maggie promises it will just be us and she won't tell the guys where we are going or who we are meeting. The last thing I need is Ryan and Darren showing up. Around 4 p.m. we leave my apartment and we start to walk to Docksides to meet up with Todd. The entire walk I didn't realize I was holding my breath until my sister tells me to breathe. When we walk in, we see that Todd is already there sitting at a high-top table in the bar area. Luckily for my sake there are plenty of people around which makes me feel better. Being in a public place guarantees he won't try to touch me again like before.

As we approach the table, Todd sees both of us and smiles like an evil cartoon villain. How have I never seen through his bullshit before? Todd stands, "Ahh, so I get both of you? I always wanted to know what it was like to be with sisters." And there it is. The first nasty comment of the evening and I am sure it won't be the last.

Maggie doesn't waste any time. "Fuck off Todd. I am only here for support. Tiffany doesn't want anything to do with you anymore. You need to leave for good and never contact her again."

Todd looks at me and cocks his head to the side, "Now Tiffy, I thought after the moment we shared in your apartment you felt the same about me as I do you."

He reaches for my hand, "Come sit down baby, let me buy you a drink." I don't respond. I don't move. I start remembering the time 3 years ago when Todd and I were celebrating a friend's birthday at a bar, similar to this one. He held my hand just to hold it under the table. He would make little circles on my palm. I remember feeling safe, loved and passionate for this man. There was a time when he was sweet but somewhere along the way that all changed, he changed, but I don't remember when.

I finally snap out of it and shake my head no, pushing him away from me, "No Todd. We are done. We have been done, since the day I found you in bed with my best friend. I am happy now without you. You need to go back to Arizona and leave me alone for good."

Todd takes a sip of beer and slams his mug on the table. Both Maggie and I jump and look around to see if anyone is paying attention to us. Nobody is.

"Look here you little tease. You are going to pack your stuff, and you will move back to Arizona with me. Julie doesn't mean shit to me. She was just a piece of ass, and if you would have listened to my needs, I wouldn't have fucked your best friend." There it is, that look... The same look in his eyes as the other day when he showed up at my apartment. He is scary and needs help before he hurts anyone. This crazy behavior and these mood swings are not normal.

"Fuck you Todd. I am only telling you one more time, and if you come near me again, I will have you arrested." I turn to Maggie and nod toward the door, "Come on Maggie, we are done here."

Maggie gets up from her chair and we both turn to leave. Todd pushes the table to get up from his seat, and his chair knocks over backwards on the floor.

"I don't think so. You are not leaving me again." Todd

reaches forward and grabs my arm. He is digging into my arm so tight that I know I am going to have bruised shape fingers on my arm. "Tiffany, I am tired of you talking back to me, you need ...."

Todd didn't get to finish his sentence. I hear a loud thud and people scream. When I open my eyes and turn around, I see Todd on the floor, his face is covered in blood and Darren is being pulled off by Ryan.

"Calm down man, he's down, okay? You knocked him out." Ryan is holding Darren back and Maggie is holding me.

I can't believe what just happened. One moment Todd is latched onto my arm, and the next he is out cold on the ground. I can't stop shivering from the shock of what just happened. Todd is still laying on the ground and people are now whispering and staring at us.

Darren turns to me and looks pissed, "Tiffany are you okay? What the fuck were you thinking?"

"I needed to put this part of my life to an end before I can move on with you. I had to tell him to leave me alone, and we are done for good. I needed closure." Tears are flowing and I can't wipe them away fast enough.

Todd is starting to regain consciousness and is wiping the blood off his face with his shirt. Darren bends down closer to Todd. "You come near her again and next time I will make sure you don't wake up." Todd doesn't say anything. He just nods his head and keeps wiping the blood that is coming out of his nose.

I have never seen Darren like this before. Well sort of. There was that time in the bar when we first met, but it was nothing like this. It stopped before it escalated. Darren leads me out the door of the restaurant and Ryan and Maggie are following right behind us.

Soon as we get outside Ryan starts yelling, "Seriously? Are you both trying to get yourself hurt? That guy is fucking crazy!" Ryan is pissed and it is hard to make him angry. He is the most chill, laidback guy I have ever met.

Maggie looks at all of us, "I know! We both know we made a bad decision. Don't be mad at Tiffany. This was my idea. I thought it would be a good way for her to move on and put the Todd issue behind her."

"Look everyone needs to please stop yelling. We need to leave before someone calls the cops though. I honestly don't think we will be seeing Todd again." I point across the street and start to walk in the direction of my apartment. "Let's go back to my place so we can talk in private."

After we settle in, the guys order a pizza and I find an ice pack for Darren's hand in the freezer. "Here, you need to put ice on it, or it will swell." I hand Darren the ice pack and he mouths Thank You.

Maggie and Ryan are sitting on the couch talking and I can't help but feel a little guilty. This is all my fault. I never should have asked Todd to meet up with me. I have some apologizing to do if I have any hope of moving on and putting this all behind me.

"Darren I am so sorry. This morning when I woke up, I freaked out. I know we talked yesterday but something felt different this morning. I panicked and I never should have left you in Savannah alone without talking to you."

Darren didn't say anything to me. He stands up, puts the

icepack down and walks toward me. With one hand he lifts my chin so I am looking at him and with the other hand he places it on the side of my head. My heart starts beating fast. He leans in to kiss me and it feels like my hearts going to pound out of my chest. It was a soft passionate kiss and it was perfect.

Ryan starts to cough and Maggie is trying not to laugh, "You guys want us to leave?" Ryan gestures towards the door and I start smiling and shake my head no.

"No, well yes but not yet. I have something to say to both of you too." Darren sits back down and puts the ice pack on his hand.

"I am sorry for running out on you guys the other day. I know you both were trying to help and not run my life. You didn't deserve that. You both are trying to plan a wedding and the last thing you need is more stress and drama. I should be helping you both not adding to your plate."

They both accept my apology and in return promise that next time they will leave it alone and not interfere. I seriously doubt that but I'll go along with it for now. After we all hug it out and say our goodbyes, they leave for the night and Darren and I are finally alone. This has been a hectic couple of days. I am mentally exhausted and I can see Darren is too.

Falling asleep in his arms is exactly what I need tonight. I lock up and start to turn out the lights. It's quiet and Darren and I haven't said anything since Maggie and Ryan left. Not because we are mad at each other but because we don't need to. The silence is nice and in some weird way we both know that this is what we need. Silence. We don't need to talk to know what we both want. Darren follows me into the bedroom and it's like we are an old married couple with our bedtime routine. We both brush our teeth, get undressed, turn out the lights and climb under the covers without saying a single word. Lying in bed together, just holding each other in silence and listening to the sound of our breathing syncing with each other. It's calming and tranquil. We eventually both drift off to sleep, putting today behind us; ready to move forward.... wherever that may take us.

CHAPTER SIXTEEN

Over the next few weeks everything seemed to be getting back to normal. Todd was non-existent, Maggie's wedding plans were about done and Darren and I were finally starting to get back to the way things were before. We were in a good place and for once I felt like all the drama and hesitance about our future was gone.

I take out a few bottles of wine from the refrigerator and get two wine glasses down from the cabinet. Maggie should be here at any moment to help plan her bachelorette party. We decided to spend the evening hashing out all the details and the guys are spending the night playing pool and having drinks at the pub down the street. I'm looking forward to this girl's trip in a few weeks. It will be nice to have some girl time and no family or boyfriend drama.

With two bottles down and working on the third bottle of wine, Maggie and I finally finish planning all the details. We decided to do a four-day all-inclusive trip to Cancun, Mexico. In exactly 3 weeks we will be laying on the beach, drinking cocktails and working on our tan. The only detail we did not hash out was making sure the guys were okay with us traveling to Mexico alone. I am a little worried about how the boys are going to handle this but Maggie assured me Ryan would be fine and Darren would eventually get on board if Ryan was.

After finishing *Project Bachelorette Party*, we start binge-watching a few hallmark movies since it's just us. I don't remember the last time we both sat down and watched a girly movie together. It was nice just her and I. We used to do this all the time when we were younger and still living at our parents' house. We were always getting in trouble for staying up too late, watching reruns of Boy Meets World on Disney. That was such a long time ago, back when the only thing we worried about was if our eye shadow looked okay and praying we didn't break out before a date.

Later that evening the guys finally stumble through the door, laughing and being too loud for it being 1 a.m. It sounds like we weren't the only ones having a nice night.

"Hey, you guys need to keep it down, I do have neighbors." I shake my head and give Maggie a look so she can help me control those two yahoos'. Not that we can do much. Maggie and I are just about as drunk as the guys.

"Hey there Peaches. I don't plan on being quiet anytime soon." Darren walks over and picks me up, tossing me over his shoulder. I squeal with excitement as he walks down the hall toward our bedroom. He gives me a nice hard smack on my ass and that's all I need to know we will not be returning for the night.

Before Darren closes our bedroom door, I yell for Maggie and Ryan to stay the night. I don't want either of them driving, they both had way too much to drink. Maggie agrees and says she will lock up before going to bed.

Darren tosses me on our bed and climbs on top of me. I'm giggling at how playful and cute he is being. He takes his shirt off and I stop laughing. The way he is looking at me right now has my entire body on fire. He slowly caresses the side of my face and kisses my neck before he starts unbuttoning my shirt. Slowly, one button at a time, so he can admire me. Making my chest more visible as he works his way down my blouse. Darren is amazing. I don't know how he can make me feel this way just by kissing and touching me but I love it. I can't wait any longer; I am craving to feel his lips on mine. I reach forward and start to kiss him. I can taste the liquor on his mouth, and I know he was drinking whiskey and ginger ale. After a few minutes of devouring each other, I need more. I need to feel his entire body pressed against mine. I need to feel the warm heat of his skin against mine.

I start licking and nibbling the side of his neck and I can taste his salty skin and feel the stubble on my tongue from his beard. I stop and move my head to one side to take a breath of air. Something feels off. I try to push him off me and rock side to side so he will move. I can't talk and start panicking. I take a few more breaths through my mouth to try and stop the feeling that I am going to throw up, but it doesn't work. I rush toward the bathroom and slam the door shut just in time to make it to the toilet.

I am not one to throw up but I cannot control my body and I violently start heaving and throwing up everything that I had earlier that day. My mind starts racing through everything I ate. Nothing tasted funny and I had nothing to eat out of the ordinary. Hopefully I just had too much to drink and it is not settling well with me. Maggie and I did have 3 bottles of wine plus we ordered Chinese for dinner. I guess the two do not go well together.

"Tiffany, are you okay? Do you need anything?" Darren tries to turn the handle, but I locked it so he couldn't come in. We are close, but I am not ready for him to see me like this yet.

"Yes, I'll be out in a few minutes. Just cleaning myself up." I stand up and start to splash water on my face. After brushing my teeth and putting my hair in a ponytail I exit the bathroom and see Darren sitting on the edge of the bed looking worried. He has a bottle of water and some aspirin next to him.

He is sweet wanting to take care of me. "Thank you. I am not sure what that was. Tomorrow I'll ask Maggie if she felt sick. The only thing I can think of is the Chinese we had for dinner."

"Well drink some water and take the aspirin. It might make you feel better. Hangovers are no fun." He hands me the water and pills and I take them.

I hate taking medicine but at this point I need something. I am still sweating and shaking and right now all I want to do is curl up in bed and sleep. I climb under the covers and turn off the light. "Good night babe. Thank you for taking care of me."

Darren moves closer and starts spooning me, rubbing the side of my arm and leg. "Good night Peaches. Try and get some rest."

The next morning, I wake up and Darren is gone. I look at the clock and it shows 10 am. Wow I must have been out of it. I can hear everyone out in the living room, so I start to get up and make sure I look presentable before heading out there. Soon as I open the bedroom door, I can smell them cooking breakfast and my stomach starts to growl. I am so thankful that I am still not sick and my appetite is back. I could use a good breakfast.

"Hey good morning, something smells delicious." I pour myself a cup of coffee and sit down at the table.

"Hey Tiff, how are you feeling? Darren said you were sick last night." Maggie looks concerned.

"Oh, I feel fine now. I think it was something I ate or maybe the combination of Chinese and wine. Who knows?" I shrug my shoulders and start to butter the toast.

Maggie stands up to bring the fruit and bacon to the table, "So I was just telling the guys about the trip to Mexico in a few weeks. They want to come too. What do you think of making it a bachelor/bachelorette trip?

Damn I was looking forward to it just being a girl's trip, but I guess having the guys there will be fun too. I know it will make Maggie more comfortable since we are going to Mexico. Especially since she has never been before.

"No not at all. That will be fun. We should call the travel agent and add them to our trip before it is too late."

I grab my cell and call the travel agent who helped us yesterday. Fifteen minutes later the guys were booked and everything was all set. I am getting really excited now. I haven't been on vacation in a while. That reminds me, I need to buy a few cute dresses and a new bathing suit for the trip. Maybe even some lingerie to surprise Darren with one night. My stomach starts to flutter. Just thinking about being alone with him at a beautiful resort gets me all worked up. This trip is going to be amazing.

"So, what does everyone have planned for today?" I hope that Maggie is free so we can go shopping.

Both of the guys have to go into work for a few hours, and Maggie said she already made plans with an old friend who is in town, so I guess it means it will be just me and my credit card today. Everyone starts to clean up and get ready for the day and I relax, finish off the rest of the bacon and coffee since everyone else is gone. I decide to take advantage of my free time and do some writing for work before calling it quits and go shopping.

It's beautiful outside and there are a bunch of cute little boutique shops all around town I want to check out. This was one thing Arizona was lacking. Everything was so commercial and you had that big city feel when you went out. I love the close-knit, small-town feel. To be honest I hated it growing up, but now that I am older and trying to settle down, this is exactly what I am looking for.

The first store I walk into was a small upscale boutique with lots of sundresses to choose from. I find three to try on. One is black with little white dots. It has a hole right below the chest area and it zips in the back. The other two are rompers. One is yellow with little flowers on it and the other is baby blue with buttons down the chest.

I try all three on and just my luck they fit perfectly. That never happens when I go shopping and find something I like. It usually fits perfect in one area but not the other. These clothes are not exactly cheap, but it's not every day I find something that fits me just right and looks great on me.

I decide to buy everything and head over to the register to check out, "Excuse me, do you know of any cute bathing suit store around here?"

The sales lady tells me there is a nice store a few blocks east if I head toward the marina. After she bags up my stuff, I start heading that way, in search of the bathing suit boutique. I want a sexy bathing suit, so when Darren sees me, he will lose his mind. That's is my goal!

The bathing suit boutique is awesome. They have every style you can think of. I find two that I like. One is all black. The top is a halter, so it pushes my breasts together and gives them that extra lift. I love how it fits. The other is a pale pink. This will look really good with a tan. The top piece is your basic triangle top but it clips in the front. The bottoms are a pattern of pale pink, white and green specs. Very tropical and sexy looking. I decide on both because I can't choose. I figure I will be there for four days and the majority of the time I will be wearing my bathing suits anyways so I will need two.

I pick up a salad on the way home and start to pack a few things I know I won't need before the trip. We're not leaving for a few weeks but I like to make sure I have everything. I turn on the music and start to eat my salad while I get everything together. I'm so in the zone and happy that I don't even here Darren come home.

"Hey beautiful, I have been calling you, are you okay?" Darren has flowers in his hands and leans down to kiss my forehead.

"Oh, I am so sorry, I had my phone on vibrate and I didn't hear it over the music. I bought a few things for the trip and have been in the zone getting it all together." I look up and smile at Darren. He's still holding the flowers and is grinning at me. He looks adorable.

"Okay, just wanted to make sure. These are for you. I'll go put them in water." He blows me a kiss and leaves the bedroom.

I finish packing what I can and head into the kitchen to see what he is doing. He is on the phone, leaning up against the kitchen counter. He holds up a finger to let me know he will be a minute. I'm in a happy playful mood so I walk over and start to kiss his neck trying to distract him from whoever he's talking to. I move my hands around to his chest and start unbuttoning his shirt; kissing his chest. I can tell he likes it and my goal to distract him seems to be working because I hear him apologizing to the person on the phone for asking them to repeat themselves.

Over the next few minutes, it turns from me being the one in control to Darren. Somehow, I end up being pushed against the counter and Darren is behind me with my dress up. The next 10 minutes is probably the hottest sex we ever had. It was so hot and intense and Darren didn't hold back when it came to vocalize what he wanted to do to me. It was like a page from those sexy erotic books I like to read. Now he has me thinking about how I want more, just like this. I loved how dominant and in charge he was.

Darren starts laughing as he helps me down off the counter, "What are you thinking about sexy?"

I start fixing my hair and dress soon as I get down, "That was so hot Darren. I mean it. Our sex life is great but this, this was amazing."

Darren looks at me for a few seconds, like he is trying to

read me so he can respond the right way.

"You enjoyed that? I was a little scared I was being too forceful with you." Darren looks a little relieved.

"Of course, I liked it. It was erotic. I loved how vocal and dominant you were. We should definitely do that again." I kiss him on the lips, tell him I am going to take a shower and that he should join me. Hopefully the shower will turn into another hot sex session where he has me begging for more.

* * *

Over the next week both of us are swamped with work and last-minute arrangements before our trip to Mexico. It's also been raining nonstop so that gives me a good jump ahead on some future articles. I am really happy I decided to shop ahead of time. I hate shopping in the rain. Maggie has been running around trying to find stuff for the trip and she keeps complaining about how she hates shopping when it storms outside. She has never been a fan of driving in the rain.

Tonight, Darren and I decide to stay in and have a pizza and movie night. It's still raining and neither of us is up for dealing with the Friday night bar crowds. I am flipping through the movie titles on the TV when the doorbell rings.

"Oh, that must be the pizza." Darren jumps up to buzz the pizza guy in and I come across the movie 50 Shades of Grey. I have never seen it before so I select the title and purchase the movie in HD with the X-rated version. Hopefully he will go along with my movie selection.

I'm a little shy when he returns a few minutes later with the food. My stomach starts to turn, and I'm second-guessing my decision when he hands me another glass of wine. Maybe I just need more liquid courage.

"Alright, the pizza smells great. Did you decide on a movie?" Darren starts scarfing his pizza waiting for me to answer him. He looks up at me and raises his eyebrows wondering why I am just staring at him. I'm still contemplating whether to tell him the movie I picked or to change it.

I smile at him and tell him I picked 50 Shades of Grey to watch. To be honest, ever since the night in the kitchen a week ago, I cannot stop thinking about sex. Not the intimate passionate sex in bed. The hot, raw, sexy kind that has you screaming and hoping the neighbors won't call the cops.

"Oh, okay, you sure?" Darren finishes his first slice and sits down next to me on the couch.

Hell yes. Darren and I haven't had sex since last week and I'm too chicken to tell him that I want him like the night in the kitchen. I have never been vocal during sex. It just doesn't come naturally for me. I feel weird and clam up. I could use the practice of saying what I want, when I want it, and how I want it. But I am not there yet, not even close. I am hoping that by us watching this movie tonight, it will be the start of just that. Hot steamy sex! I press play and grab my wine. Darren kisses me on my forehead and clinks his glass with mine, cheering us to a nice Friday night. One can only hope!

CHAPTER SEVENTEEN

Finally, today is the day. Cancun here we come. I am sitting on my bed repacking my suitcase for the fifth time. I want to make sure none of my clothes are wrinkled, not to mention I don't want to forget anything. As I repack, my mind starts to drift off to Darren and I having hot sex. I swear lately it's like all I can think about. I heard about women's sex drives increasing after 30 but I am only 26. I seriously doubt that is what's happening here, plus I think that is just a myth.

Last week when Darren and I started watching 50 Shades of Grey, all I hoped for was at some point we would start having hot steamy sex. To be honest that was the entire reason I wanted to watch the movie, and lucky me, it worked. We lasted halfway through the movie before we started having sex right there on the coffee table. Darren ripped my favorite blouse off me and buttons went everywhere. One even flew into my wine. It was probably one of the best sex nights we ever had. Every caress and kiss made my body burst beyond anything I could ever imagine.

"Hello, earth to Tiffany. Come in Tiffany." Maggie was standing in front of me looking annoyed.

"Hey, I am almost done. I just need to put a few more items in my suitcase and I will be done." I am embarrassed so I start shoving the remaining articles of clothing into my suitcase.

"What in the hell were you just thinking about? You looked about a mile away?" Maggie sits on the edge of my bed and starts helping me put the clothes away.

"I was just daydreaming about laying on the beach." I can feel my cheeks getting red so I stand up and zip the suitcase back up.

"Right sure, maybe daydreaming about you guys having sex on the beach. You were completely off in la-la land Tiffany. Hurry up we need to leave in 10 minutes." Maggie laughs as she leaves my room.

Wow, was I in that deep of thought where I didn't even hear her come into my room and start talking to me? Man, I don't know what's with me. I grab my suitcase and start to wheel it out of my room. Everyone else is in the living room waiting patiently but Maggie looks like she a bomb that's about to detonate at any moment.

Maggie has always had high anxiety when it comes to traveling or being on time. I blame that on my mom and her checklist system. I like to be prepared and organized but I don't have the added anxiety as my sister does. Thankfully.

* * *

We sit down and buckle are seat belts just before the flight attendant comes on the line to tell us this will be a full flight. I cannot wait until we are up in the air and I can order a drink. I need a glass of wine bad. My sister is driving me crazy. I forgot how much I hate traveling with her. I try to tune out my sister while I listen to the flight attendants go over the safety precautions but there is no use.

"Maggie, please calm down. You did not forget anything and even if you did, we are going to Mexico, we can get whatever you need." I try my best to ease her anxiety but it's almost damn near impossible. Her legs are bouncing up and down and she is glaring out the window while chewing on her thumbnail. I look over at Ryan and shrug. There is no hope at this point. We just need to let her do what she needs to do to calm herself down.

Twenty minutes later I can see the flight attendants starting to move around the cabin, and I know that means drinks will be available shortly. When it's our rows turn, I decide to start with my maid of honor duties and I order everyone a glass of champagne so we can start to celebrate.

I hand everyone their champagne when it arrives and I start my toast. Hopefully this takes Maggie's focus off from flying and puts her in a better mood.

"Cheers to Maggie and Ryan. I am so happy you both found each other. I couldn't imagine you two finding someone more compatible to spend the rest of your life with. Cheers to an amazing bachelor/bachelorette party. I love you both so much!"

We clink our glasses and Maggie finally starts to relax.

Success! The flight isn't bad. It's only about 3 hours long, so we use that time to talk about what excursions we would like to do and what fun things the resort has to offer. The resort has 5 restaurants which all sound delicious, 3 giant pools, 1 being an adult-only pool. I am excited to try that pool out. It says you can be naked and there are no phones or recording devices allowed. I get butterflies in my stomach just thinking about the possibility of laying naked by the pool. Although I doubt that it will happen since my sister and future brother in law will be there but a girl can fantasize.

"You know one of the excursions is a catamaran. It takes us out in the ocean, sails for 3 hours, plays music and they have complimentary rum punch. I think they even stop on a little private beach for a bit. That might be fun." Everyone agrees on the Catamaran tour and we decide to book it when we check into the hotel.

The rest of the plane ride isn't bad. Maggie and Ryan both snuggle and whisper stuff to each other. It's like they are oblivious that anyone else is around. Darren and I both close our eyes and rest until we hear the captain come on to tell us we are almost here and to buckle our seat belts.

As the plane starts to descend into Cancun's airport, you can tell everyone is excited and ready to start this vacation. It's finally here! No more plans or countdowns leading up to the trip. No drama, no ex-fiancé or work to get in the way. Just the four of us in an all-inclusive resort with no worries.

After we get off the plane, Maggie and I use the restroom while the guys wait for our bags. I refuse to use the airplane bathrooms if I can help it. That little three by three closet of a bathroom freaks me out and unless I need to, I will wait until we land. I have watched Snakes on a Plane, and there is no way I am locking myself in a small bathroom. By the time we make it off the plane, I am ready to explode, so we both make a mad dash to the restroom. I could hear the guys laughing as we take off together.

"Tiffany, I am so happy we are here together. Thank you for helping me plan this bachelor/bachelorette trip. I know originally it was supposed to be just the two of us, but I think the guys will make the trip even more fun." Maggie looks guilty but I am not sure why.

"I agree Maggie. Completely. You don't need to feel bad that they are here. I am so excited too." I reach over and hug Maggie as she finishes washing her hands. She turns around and flicks the water from her hands at me and we both start laughing.

"Okay, okay, let's go find the guys before we get into a water battle in the middle of the bathroom." We are still laughing when we find the guys at the baggage claim area.

The guys grab all the bags and we start heading outside to the curb to find our shuttle service. The drive to our hotel is amazing and the views along the coast take your breath away. The water is so blue and tropical. Maggie is glued to the window looking at all the beautiful resorts and homes as we drive by.

Darren takes advantage of Ryan and Maggie being distracted by the scenery, and he starts kissing my neck and whispering into my ear. "I cannot wait to get you alone Peaches." Darren starts to tickle my neck. I have never been a huge fan of PDA but with Darren it never seems to bother me. If we go a while without touching each other, I start to crave the feeling of his skin touching mine.

I look over at him and I don't need to say a word. He knows

exactly how I feel. He kisses me a few more times before the shuttle stops, bringing us both back to reality. We are finally at the resort! Maggie and I jump out while the guys help unload the luggage. I start to head into the lobby to get checked in while Maggie makes sure all the luggage is accounted for and gets the luggage tickets.

The resort is amazing. Everything is open and the floors and walls are white marble with white sheer curtains blowing in the wind that leads out to the pool area. There is a small fishpond in the middle of the lobby and a bar off to the right. I finally make my way over to the front desk to get us settled in and luckily there is no line. This is starting off perfectly.

"Hola. Checking in please." Maggie walks up next to me just in time and we both hand our hotel confirmations to the lady behind the desk.

She smiles and hands us both a complimentary drink, "Hola, Senoritas. Welcome to Cancun." After she finishes checking us in, she hands us our wrist bands, room cards, and a map. She explains that there are 5 restaurants in the resort, live entertainment each night and all the bars are open until 2 am, except for the adult pool bar, which is open all the time.

"Gracias." We turn to see if we can locate the guys, and sure enough they are at the lobby bar ordering us drinks. We hurry up and finish the complimentary drink we were given and walk over.

"Hey guys, you must have read our minds." Maggie takes the drinks from Ryan and hands me mine. "Okay, so why don't we go check out our rooms, and then let's meet back here so we can head to the pool. Say 20 minutes?"

My eyes light up. I cannot wait to get Darren alone. "Works

for us, See you guys soon."

We bring our drinks with us and we all pile into the elevator. Maggie and Ryan get off on the 4th floor, and we stay on. We are on the 5th floor. I could have sworn we booked our rooms so they were close together.

After the doors close, Darren smiles. "Okay, I called yesterday and upgraded our room to a Jacuzzi suite."

"Are you serious?" I start jumping up and down. Luckily, I already finished my Margarita or it would have gone everywhere.

The room is amazing. The view overlooks the pools and has a perfect view of the ocean. The Jacuzzi is huge and I think I could float on my back, it's that big. I cannot wait to try that out tonight.

Thirty minutes later, we make it down to the lobby where I see Ryan and Maggie having another drink at the bar. Maggie looks so cute in her new bathing suit holding her frozen drink. I am so happy for her. She deserves this trip and I want to make sure she has the best time.

"Hey, guys sorry we are a few minutes late. We got a little distracted." I start laughing but it turns into a squeal when Darren smacks my ass.

"Yea we did." Darren laughs and picks me up, lifting me over his shoulder. "Come on let's go to the pool."

Everyone is cracking up and I am still hanging over Darren's left shoulder as we walk out. Darren finally sets me down when we make it to the pool. We all just stand there and admire how tropical and serene everything is. It's like a picture-perfect day. Not a cloud in the sky, the pool isn't busy and there is music playing in the background. I couldn't have dreamed up a more perfect setting.

I break up the silence, "Okay smart ass, now go get us a drink, and we'll find us some chairs." I kiss Darren and find us chairs to lay our towels on. The pool looks so refreshing so I jump in and wait for him to bring us our drinks back.

Maggie and Ryan are sitting on the edge of the pool and I am in the water when Darren returns. He quickly hops in to join me and hands me my drink.

"Okay so the bartender said that the Japanese restaurant here is amazing. Do you want to go there for dinner tonight?" Darren holds his drink up and dunks his head under the water.

We all look at each other in agreement to go to the Japanese restaurant tonight. It sounds delicious and my stomach starts to rumble. I completely forgot that I haven't eaten anything since early this morning. We're all having such a good time, so I decide not to mention lunch right now but I know I'll have to find a snack to eat soon.

Over the next few hours we hang out and drink in the pool. The pool bar has chips and salsa that we start snacking on and opt-out of taking a break for lunch. The music is loud, everyone is laughing and having a good time and it starts getting entertaining when the staff brings out games for the guests to play. They do a blindfolded water balloon contest. That's was hilarious. The guys tried to get us to participate but we refused. They also had a hairy chest competition and a belly flop contest. I rather watch on the sidelines and not be the entertainment for others.

Around 5:00 pm we all decide to call it quits and go get ready for dinner. I'm glad because the last hour I started feeling a little nauseous and choose to drink only bottled water. The elevator ride doesn't help. I keep breathing in through my nose to help control the urge of throwing up.

"Tiffany, are you sure you are okay? You look pale." Maggie feels my forehead but I don't have a fever.

I reassure her I will be okay and we plan to meet at the lobby bar at 7 pm. Soon as we reach our floor and the doors open, I rush out and run to my room. Darren can't open the door fast enough. I just make it to the toilet before I throw up the last 4 hours of Margaritas and chips and salsa. Oh no. I cannot be getting sick right now.

"Here eat this, it will help settle your stomach. Between drinking, and not eating, you are probably just getting dehydrated." Darren finds some granola and bottled water in our refrigerator and hands it to me.

"Thank you, babe." I feel so guilty. It's our first night and he is taking care of me like a child.

After I finish eating the granola bar, I start to feel better. I guess I just need something in my stomach. I jump in the shower and start getting ready so we're not late for dinner. In the shower I start thinking about feeling sick. I also felt sick last week too. To be honest, I haven't been feeling like myself for some time now. I get out of the shower and start to dry off, when I get this sick/scared feeling in the pit of my stomach.

"Oh no, no, no, no." I start whispering to myself. I try to backtrack when was the last time I had my period, and I can't remember. Crap. This cannot be possible. We have been really careful. And then it dawns on me, the night Darren came to Savannah. We did not use anything. Oh no. I cannot be pregnant, we haven't been dating for that long. But deep down, I think I know the truth; I am pregnant. I must be. Why else would I keep throwing up and getting nauseous for no reason? My boobs have been sore too but I just figured it was from working out the last couple of weeks in preparation for the trip and wedding.

I finish drying off and step out of the bathroom. I must have looked like I saw a ghost or something. Darren stops dead in his tracks and stares at me. I can tell he's trying to see if I'm still sick or what.

"Peaches, what's wrong? You still feel sick?" Darren walks over and sits down next to me on our bed.

"Ummm, no I actually feel a little better but I realized something while I was in the shower." I look down afraid to say anymore. We never discussed kids or the possibility of us getting pregnant. What if he doesn't want kids or decides to bail out?

"Okay, what's wrong?" Darren stands up and finishes buttoning his shirt. He's standing in front of me but looking down so he can both look at me and the holes on his shirt while he buttons them.

"I am late. I think I might be pregnant." I don't know to ease into it or how to say it, so I just blurt it out before I change my mind and chicken out.

Darren stops and his head jerks up. Our eyes meet but neither one of us says a word. Now he looks like he has seen a ghost. I realize I should say something else but I don't know what to say or what to do.

Darren walks over and kneels so he is facing me. He puts his arms on both sides of me and looks up. "Are you sure? When you say late, are you talking a few days? Maybe it's just all the stress you have been through lately."

I wish that was the case but no. I shake my head no, "I haven't had my period since before I went dress shopping. That was over 6 weeks ago."

"Okay, well before we both freak out, let's find out for sure." Darren stands up and finishes getting dressed. He grabs his wallet and heads to the door.

"Wait, where are you going?" I stand up, worried. I'm not even close to ready to leave yet for dinner.

"Finish getting ready. I am going to run down to the lobby for a moment. I will be right back." Darren blows me a kiss and leaves. How can he be so calm and nonchalant at a time like this?

I walk back into the bathroom and finish my makeup. I know I won't have time to blow dry my hair so I decided to go with the beachy wet look and put mousse in my hair to hold the wave. Just as I finish zipping up my sundress, Darren walks in with a bag.

"Hey, babe come here." He walks into the bathroom and puts the bag on the counter.

I follow him with a confused look on my face but I don't ask what he is doing, I just wait to hear what he has to say.

"Look before we know for sure whether you are pregnant, I want you to know that if you are, I mean we are, that I am here. I am not going anywhere. I have always wanted kids and I love you." Darren smiles and pulls a pregnancy test out of the bag.

My heart starts pounding and my palms are sweating. I don't know if I am ready to find out yet. I smile and take the test from him. "I am scared Darren."

"I know, but we can do this. There is nothing to be scared about." Darren hugs me and opens the package.

"Okay. I guess I need to know now, especially since we are on vacation." We both head to the bathroom and I sit down and pee on the stick. Usually I would make Darren leave while I use the bathroom but I don't want to be alone, and to be honest I doubt he would leave anyway.

I place the cap on the test and finish washing my hand. "It said to wait 3 minutes."

Darren jumps up and sits on the bathroom counter, swinging his legs back and forth like he is a kid waiting for the ice cream truck to arrive. He looks adorably calm and patient. Neither of us talks in the 3 minutes we are waiting. He just smiles and stares at me. I can't believe we are both here waiting to find out if we are going to be parents. Talk about a shocker. If I had to bet someone this morning when we were leaving for Cancun that this is how my night would end, I would have lost without a doubt.

My phone starts buzzing and we know it's time. Deep down I don't need this test to know. I can feel it in my gut that I am pregnant. Darren picks up the test and holds it in his hand. He looks down at the pregnancy test but his facial expression doesn't change. Damn he has a good poker face. What the hell am I pregnant or not?

"Darren." I put my hand on his and he looks up at me. Darren continues to smile.

"Tiffany, you are no longer allowed to drink on this trip. You are pregnant sweetheart." He hands me the test to see for myself and jumps down off the counter.

Darren gives me a hug and a kiss. "It will be okay Tiffany. I promise. We will do this together."

I know everything will be okay but I don't think I have ever been this nervous before. I kiss Darren back and hug him. "I love you Darren. Thank you for being so calm and okay with this. It really makes it easier for me to handle it all."

We both finish getting ready and are only 5 minutes late for meeting Ryan and Maggie for dinner. While we head down to the lobby we discuss if we are going to tell them. I don't want to, only because this is their trip and I don't want to take this special time away but Darren wants to tell everyone. After a little begging he agrees to keep it a secret and to help with the secret, I will keep drinking but order virgin drinks to hide the fact I am pregnant. This should be interesting and I hope we can pull it off. I want this trip to be all about Maggie and Ryan and not Tiffany and her new drama of the week.

CHAPTER EIGHTEEN

"Yes, I will have a strawberry daiquiri, please." I smile at the waiter and he gives me a wink.

Darren had pulled the hostess aside when we first arrived and told her anytime I order a drink tonight it must be with no alcohol, and to keep it between us. I guess this hasn't been the first request like this because she agreed without questioning and even congratulated me. This might work after all and get away with our little secret on this trip.

We are having a great time. The food is amazing, the entertainment has us laughing and I almost forgot I was pregnant until Maggie started shoving sushi at me.

"Here Tiffany try this. It's awesome." Maggie pushes the plate toward me and I nicely push it back, shaking my head.

"I am good for now, thank you though." The thought of sushi makes my stomach turn a little, let alone the fact that I can't eat raw fish when I'm pregnant.

She gives me a weird look but doesn't ask questions. I never turn down sushi. I love sushi. Maybe I should say something.

"I am full, and I don't want to overeat and feel sick again." I am hoping she understands. Maggie seems to get it and doesn't push it any further, so I don't bring it up or stress over it anymore. The dessert however is a different story. Darren orders a double fudge chocolate cake and I sneak a few bites. It is so delicious and I almost order another one because I can't stop eating his.

After dinner we all decide to go walk around the resort and check out the different areas. We only got to the hotel about 7 hours ago and the majority of the time was spent in the main pool. We see a sign for the adult pool and spa and decide to check it out. I have been waiting to come here since the plane ride to check it out.

We follow the sign and it leads us down a little path. Its lined with trees and exotic flowers to make it feel more secluded than the rest of the place. When we arrive, there are a few people in the pool and some laying on the lounge chairs. Everyone is naked and I am not sure why I am shocked, but I am. I want to stay and go swimming but I can tell Maggie is a little uncomfortable because after she peeks over the gate, she turns around and asks where to go next like she isn't fazed by all the nudists.

We follow her back down the pathway to the main area. Darren can tell that I wanted to stay so he squeezes my hand to let me know we will come back for sure. I smile without turning to him. I love how connected we are. Lately we have been on point with each other and it makes me feel even closer than usual to him.

After walking around the resort and checking out where the

other restaurants, pools, beach access and indoor spa is, I decide to call it a night and Darren and I head back to our room. Ryan and Maggie decide they are going to stay out and have a few drinks and listen to music at the bar. I cannot wait to get my wedges off. My feet are killing me. I take my shoes off in the elevator and moan in relief of how good it feels. I don't care how this may look to others, my feet are swollen and I need to relax.

"I cannot wait to feel how comfortable this bed is. I am exhausted." The doors open and I walk out toward our room. Darren opens the door for me and soon as I make it in the room, I am lifting my dress over my head and crawling on top of our bed. It's a huge king size bed and just as I hoped, so comfortable.

"Wow you are not wasting any time, huh?" Darren slowly unbuttons his pants and lets them drop to the floor as he pulls his shirt over his head.

I watch him closely as he walks towards the bed and climbs in next to me. God this man is so sexy. I don't know how I got this lucky. Darren climbs on top of me and starts kissing me. He doesn't ask, doesn't start slow, he just starts kissing me, or devouring me is more like it. He puts one of his arms under my back to lift me slightly and I arch forward pushing my breasts into his chest.

I have heard that sex feels better when you are pregnant and your body is more sensitive but holy crap. Darren's body feels like it is on fire. His skin is so hot and I love it. He keeps teasing me by rubbing the sides of my thighs and I can't take it anymore. Every touch of him feels too good and I need him now.

"Maybe I should tease you a little more." Darren continues to massage me and I feel like I can't wait any longer.

I thought the kitchen sex was good, but oh my God. Darren starts slow, taking it easy before moving faster. I begin to match him, and my hips move with his. I control the tempo and grind into him faster and faster until Darren takes over.

Darren pushes my arms into the mattress and his breathing is heavy. He leans forward and starts kissing my ear, "You feel amazing."

That does it for me. My orgasm has been building and I can't control the urge any longer. Darren moves faster and faster until we both start crying out and release at the same time. This was indescribable. How two people can have sex and it feels this good is beyond me. I am all ready for round two but I know Darren is exhausted. He flips over onto his back, still panting like he ran a marathon.

I lean on my side and start rubbing his chest with my nails. I love this man more than anything in the world.

"God, baby. Do you have any idea what you do to me?" Darren looks over at me and blows me a kiss with his lips. I blow him a kiss back and lay my head down on my pillow. I continue to rub his chest and within 5 minutes I can hear his breathing change. He drifted off to sleep. I start to close my eyes too, and the sound of him exhaling puts me right to sleep in no time.

* * *

The next few days are a blur. This trip went by way too fast and I am sad when we have to leave. Everything from the resort, to the food, and the hot amazing sex was more than I anticipated. We all vouch that we will come back again, and soon. Being pregnant on this trip was a breeze and honestly, I cannot believe how easy it was to hide it from everyone. Maggie didn't ask questions or give me weird looks. It did help that she was in her own little world and enjoying her bachelorette trip. It made it easy to keep the focus on her and Ryan and off from me and my secret.

On the plane, we are all quiet and don't talk much. I think between us being tired and not looking forward to returning to our normal lives, we all take the time to relax. I fell asleep a few times and each time I dreamt about being pregnant and having a baby. It has felt like a fantasy up until this point. Now when we return home, it's going to feel more real. Especially since I will have to start telling people and making plans on what to do next.

The thought of actually telling others is enough to keep me awake for the rest of the flight home. My anxiety starts to kick in a little and I start picking at my nails. A habit I didn't even realize I had until Darren pointed it out to me. I thought Maggie was the only one with that nervous habit.

Darren grabs my hand to stop me from peeling off all my nails, "Talk to me. What's on your mind Tiffany. Is it the baby?"

I give him a guilty smile. I hope he doesn't think I don't want the baby because I do. I'm starting to come to terms with the idea of us being a family. I am just freaked. Everything is happening so fast. Not long ago I was engaged to an asshole who I left, I traveled across the country back home, and now I am having a baby with my boyfriend who I have only been dating for a few months.

"Yea. I am just nervous, still a little shocked and not sure what to do next." It feels good to be able to be open and honest with him. I could never do that with Todd. He always made me feel like an idiot.

"Soon as we get home, we will sit down and make some plans, okay? Everything will be fine." He kisses me on my forehead and I relax a little.

I can do this. We can do this. I start making a mental checklist in my head. I will need a bigger apartment, I have to make a doctor's appointment, and figure out when to tell my parents and Maggie. God, my parents are going to be shocked. Darren and I just told them a few weeks ago we were dating. Then it hits me. I have no idea who Darren's parents are. He never really has talked about them. He's mentioned little things here and there but overall nothing major. The only thing I know is that he is from Georgia. How have I never picked up on this or thought about it until now? I start to panic and realize that I am living with a guy and all I know is his name is Darren Hart, he is from Georgia, and he works for an investment company.

I turn to Darren and tap him on his shoulder. "Darren, how come we never talk about your family? I have no idea about your life. Isn't that a little strange?"

Darren shrugs, "I never thought about it, I guess. What do you want to know?"

He never thought about it. That's his response? How can you never think about your family and life back home?

"I want to know everything. I mean we have been dating now for a little over 3 months, and we are having a baby together. I think now is as good as time as any to start thinking about it. Right?"

Darren is about to say something when the flight attendant

comes over the intercom and advises we are about to land and to return our seats to the upright position. I decide to let it go for now. I don't want to have this conversation on the plane where someone can overhear us. Especially Maggie and Ryan who are sitting in the row in front of us.

* * *

The ride home is weird. Everyone is quiet. Ryan and Maggie drop us off, we say our goodbyes and head inside to our apartment. I start to unpack and make piles of clothes for laundry and Darren orders us some pizza. I keep replaying our conversation in my head repeatedly while I sort through the clothes. I want to bring it back up again but I don't want to seem needy.

"Are you going to sort the same pile of clothes for the third time?" Darren snaps me out of my trans and I look up at him. He's smiling and gestures toward the kitchen.

"Okay Peaches. Let's talk over pizza." He puts a slice of pizza on a plate for me and sits it down on the table.

I walk into the kitchen to grab us some bottled water and when I return, he has a weird look on his face. A look like he is about to tell me something but he's afraid of my reaction.

"Okay so where should we start?" I hand him the water and I sit down. I feel weird like we are on a first date and we are about to quiz each other. I know we don't know a whole lot about each other but that was what was nice. Not having the stress and drama of dealing with it. But now maybe that wasn't the smartest idea.

"Okay well you already know I am from Georgia and my

folks still live there. I am the only child. My parents are still together and they are happy. We live right outside of Savannah." Darren takes a few bites of his pizza before continuing.

I'm listening to him and eating my pizza. So far this is stuff I already know through previous conversations.

"The investment company I work for, H & H Solutions, my family owns that company. My grandfather started it, my dad joined the business when he was 18, and I joined when I was 18."

I can't believe I didn't know this. I mean I knew he worked for an investment company called H & .. something, but I had no idea he worked for his dad, and his family owned the business.

"Wow that's awesome. I had no idea you worked for your family. So, you run the office here I guess?" I am really interested. I think this is amazing that he is fortunate enough to be in the family business.

"Ummm, well I don't exactly work for them Tiffany. I own half the business. I started learning about the business when I was 16. When I turned 18, I started working there, attending board meetings, and I received my share in the company stock when I turned 21 and graduated from college. When my grandfather passed away 5 years ago, he left me his part of the company. I own half the business with my father."

I am at a loss for words. I cannot believe I did not know this. How could I have not known this? Why would he want to keep this from me? If I owned my own company, I would be happy to tell people about my family's success.

"Okay so you own H & H Solutions and it's an investment company. What do you guys invest in?" I grab my phone and start to google H & H Solutions while Darren starts to explain his company to me.

"We invest in startup businesses; we also buy out companies that are in financial ruin and either try to repair them or we sell them off. We look for companies that are up and comers and we can help launch." Darren looks at me and I can hear him cough when I don't reply.

I am staring at my phone I cannot believe what I am reading. His family is The Hart family. How have I never put this together? His family has invested in companies such as Ride Inc, MovieStream, and even a few major hospitals. I glance up at Darren.

"Wait you are.... No way. Your dad is Johnathan Hart?" I am speechless. His family his huge. Not only do they own the most popular rideshare company, but they also own the streaming company that started the idea of watching movies and shows on TV using an app.

"Look, please don't think I was hiding this from you. I wanted to tell you. I just have a hard time. Ever since I was a kid, everyone treated me differently because of my family and who they were. I wanted to meet friends and find someone who didn't know my background first." Darren looks different. He looks vulnerable like he just told me his deepest, darkest secret and I guess in some way he has.

"Wow, Darren I had no idea. I don't know what to say. Of course, I am not mad. I guess I understand why you would wait to tell me or anyone for that matter. Growing up in the spotlight like that must have been challenging." I want to ask Darren but I am afraid he is going to think I care, because I don't. I have never been that person that cares about money. But being the owner of such a large company like that, he must have money.

Darren must have seen the wheels turning because I didn't have to ask him. The next thing out of his mouth was exactly that.

"Okay so anyways, let's talk money because I have it. I have a lot, more than I will ever need in my entire life. So, when I told you in Cancun everything will be okay, it will be. Not just because I am not going anywhere, but financially, we are set." Darren finishes his pizza and leans back on the chair. I can see he is trying to read me. He is trying to see how I am processing all this information.

"Okay, well congrats on all the money and all, but Darren that was never an issue I was worried about. I make good money as a writer. So even if you didn't make much, I knew we would be okay." That is the truth. I have never worried about money and never understood how people can let money change them.

Darren doesn't say anything. He just sits there and stares at me. Finally, he smiles, "Okay Tiffany good. I mean I never thought you would have an issue, but I am glad to know that the money thing doesn't freak you out."

Darren stands up and puts our plates in the sink. "There is one more thing though. My parents do know about you. I told them last month that I was dating someone and she is a beautiful intelligent writer from North Carolina. They cannot wait to meet you."

My head snaps up. "They want to meet me. Why?" I feel like an idiot as the words left my mouth. Of course, his parents want to meet the person he's dating. I just wasn't expecting that they already knew about me.

Darren looks confused, "Well, we have been dating for over 3 months now, and I always talk about you. I guess they want to see who I fell in love with."

I feel like going to be sick. In the last 5 days, I have found out a lot of information in a short amount of time. First, I find out I am pregnant while on vacation in Cancun, then my boyfriend owns H & H Solutions and he has more money than he knows what to do with. Now his parents want to meet me, and they have known about me now for a month. This is all too much and I need to lay down. I feel nauseous and it is not from being pregnant this time. On top of it all, Maggie is getting married in 2 weeks. I don't know how I am going to handle all this and not tell her what's going on. I need someone to vent to and tell me everything will be okay. And the one person I need to tell, I can't.

CHAPTER NINETEEN

I haven't been able to sleep the last few nights. Finding out I'm pregnant and Darren is the owner of a multibillion-dollar company is a lot to take all at once. I get why he didn't tell me, but I wish he did. He could have at least eased into it over the last few months. I get it's not just something you throw out there, but we have been dating a while now. If I didn't push him to open up, I don't know when he would have told me. I don't care about money. I care about him being honest with me. What else is he not telling me?

"Babe, you okay? You keep tossing around in your sleep." Darren nudges me a little to get my attention.

I sit up in bed. I cannot take this anymore. We need to talk and clear the air. I am confused and upset and have so many questions.

"Darren, why did you feel like you had to keep who you are a secret from me? Did you not trust me?"

I don't know how else to say it so I just blurt it out. I look at him and I can tell he is just as upset as I am.

"No, I promise I wanted to tell you. It has nothing to do with me thinking I cannot trust you or anything. It's just I have been burned before, and I wanted us to get to know each other before you found out what I did for a living and who my family was. Growing up, all my friends and girlfriends were in my life because of my name. I am just more careful now who I open up to these days."

Darren looks sincere and I feel horrible. I can't imagine growing up like that, not knowing who your real friends are. That must have sucked.

"Thank you for telling me now. I love you and it has nothing to do with your job or your family. It has everything to do with who you are as a person and how you make me feel." I move closer to Darren and kiss him on his cheek before I lay my head on his bare chest. I can feel his heart pounding away. I know this wasn't easy for him to do. I just hope he does trust me as much as he says he does.

"Tiffany, my parents have known about you for a month now. They know we have been dating for almost 3. I promise they want to meet you. And now that we are having a baby, now is as good of a time as any." Darren takes a deep breath and waits for me to respond.

I am petrified of meeting his parents. What if they don't like me, or worse what if they think I am trying to trap their son.

"Darren, I don't know. We have Maggie and Ryan's wedding in 2 weeks and besides, I am nervous. The first time I meet your parents we are also telling them I am pregnant. I don't know if I can do that." I get up and start putting on my robe.

"Why are you nervous Peaches? They will love you. Please talk to me." Darren gets up out of bed and follows me across the room.

"I promise, my parents will adore you just as I do." He leans in and gives me a soft kiss on my lips.

"What if your parents think I am trying to trap you or something. They don't know that I just found out about you." There I finally said it. I am cringing inside, afraid to hear what Darren will say to that.

Instead, he starts cracking up laughing. Now I am really confused. "I don't understand why you think this is funny. I am serious." I slap Darren on the arm, and now I am laughing but I think mine might be more of a nervous laugh than anything.

"Okay good, because I invited my parents to come to visit this weekend so they can get to know you." Darren gives me a cute guilty but don't hate me grin and starts to back away as if he's afraid of setting me off.

"You did what? Darren you can't just drop stuff like that on me." I start to pace back and forth. Okay now I am starting to freak out. I mean what does he expect. He already knows my parents and they know him.

"Maybe we should hold off to tell them we are having a baby for a few more weeks. I think dropping that on both of our families is a little too much to take right now." I am praying Darren agrees. That will at least help me get through the next few weeks.

Darren starts to walk into the bathroom, "Okay, I think

that's a good idea. I promise you Tiffany, they will love you."

He shuts the door and I can hear him start the shower. Good, I need some time to myself to take all this in.

* * *

I start to throw everything I own out of my closet. I hate all my clothes. Nothing is fitting right. I want to look respectable and beautiful for his parents today, but none of my clothes look right. I try on my purple flower sundress. It's my last hope. I remember this one has always been a little big so I am praying that it fits.

"Yes, thank you baby, it fits." I start dancing in circles when Darren walks in and interrupts my happy dance.

"Hey beautiful, are you almost ready? I told my parents we would meet them at their hotel for brunch in 20 minutes." Darren taps his watch and gives me the look. The kind of look like your parents gave you when you were a kid and they were threatening to leave you if you didn't get in the car.

"Yes, I am ready, just putting on my shoes." I start panicking. I know they were here just a second ago.

I start throwing up the clothes that are laying on the floor. I can't find them anywhere. Crap. I rush into my closet, hoping they are sitting on my shelf. Damn it! I can't make him late on the day he is introducing me to his parents. I hear him cough a few times. I know he is starting to get impatient so I grab the closest pair of shoes and walk out.

Darren is standing there holding my strappy brown sandals by his middle finger and laughing.

"Tiffany. Sit down. You need to relax. Here are your shoes."
I follow his orders and sit on the bed. I take a deep long breath and
start to put my shoes on. I hate it when he is right. I am losing my
mind. It's just his parents, two people just like us. I will be fine. I
grab my purse and motion toward the door for us to leave.

The car ride to the hotel is quiet. I can tell Darren is
thinking about how this visit will go. He looks deep in thought so I
decide not to interrupt him. Within 15 minutes we are pulling up
and the Valet opens my door to help me get out of the vehicle.
Darren hands the valet the keys and takes the ticket.

"Okay baby, let's go have brunch with my parents." He
guides me towards the door by pushing on my lower back. Soon as
we enter the lobby, I am amazed. It's beautiful, with large ceilings,
rustic beams and beautiful art hanging on the wall. This place must
be expensive. This hotel hosts the best brunch spot in North
Carolina, and they are known for their Eggs Benedict and Steak.

Darren motions towards the restaurant and we start to walk
toward the door. We barely take 10 steps and I hear a woman yell
Darren's name. We both spin around and see his parents walking
toward us from the lobby desk. His mother is extremely pretty and
his father looks just like Darren, just older. More seasoned. They
are both very attractive and I can see parts of Darren in both of his
parents.

"Mom, Dad, there you are. I thought you would be sitting
down by now." Darren leans in to give both his parents a hug. His
mother holds on to him making his dads separate the two so he can
hug Darren. It's really sweet, I can tell she misses her son.

"Mom, Dad, this is Tiffany, my girlfriend. Tiffany this is my mother, Marisa and my dad, Jonathan." Darren motions to both of his parents as he introduces us.

"Good morning, Mr. and Mrs. Hart, it's a pleasure to meet you." I go in for a handshake, but his dad laughs and pulls me in for a hug. His mother shakes her head and does the same.

"Nonsense dear, we hug in this family." Darren's mom lets me go and looks me up and down.

"Tiffany, you are so pretty sweetheart. And I love that dress. It's a perfect brunch dress for today." His mother is sweet and she is beaming from ear to ear. She looks genuinely happy to see us both. Maybe this won't be so bad after all.

Mr. Hart starts to move toward the restaurant and we all follow him inside. As we are being seated, Darren fills his parents in on work and asks how their flight was to North Carolina. The waiter comes over and fills our water glasses and asks what we would all like to drink. Right away, Mrs. Hart speaks up and orders a round of mimosas for the table. Before I can say anything, Darren speaks up and tells his parents that I am getting over a stomach bug so Champagne might not be the best thing for me.

"Oh, please Darren, let her be. She looks fine." Mrs. Hart turns toward me and rolls her eyes, "I swear, don't let them make all the decisions for you. I had to put my foot down with this one a while ago." She motions to Mr. Hart, and they both start laughing.

The waiter returns to the table with four mimosas and places them down in front of all of us. Darren gives me an apologetic look. I know he feels bad, but I am okay. It's weird. If I'd known this would have happened 2 hours ago, I probably would have freaked out and refused to go. His parents are nice. There is something about them that makes you feel at ease.

We all order our food and I talk about my career as a writer and journalist. I talk about my family and how my sister is getting married in a little over a week, and we are both in the wedding. Brunch is going great and we are all laughing and getting along. Darren mentions that he will be traveling to Georgia in a few weeks for some business meetings, and his parents even insist I come too so we can all spend a long weekend together. I can't believe how nervous I was, and for nothing.

Darren's mom notices I haven't touched my Champagne and motions to the menu. "Tiffany, dear, if you don't like mimosa's you are welcome to order something else."

"Oh, thank you Mrs. Hart. I am honestly fine with the lemon water though." I smile and I try to think of something to change the subject but I can't think of anything. I decide to excuse myself and go to the restroom.

I walk into the restroom and admire the décor and ambiance of the room. It's beautiful and I can't help think that they probably host nice weddings here too. There is a strong smell of cleaner as I approach the bathroom and it immediately makes my stomach turn. I try taking a few deep breaths but it only makes it worse. I know I am not going to be able to keep my food down so I rush into the stall and start throwing up my steak and eggs immediately. Yuck, how can it taste so good but taste so bad coming back up? I hear someone open the door and wash their hands. I try to be as quiet as I can but I know they can hear me. I wipe my mouth with some toilet paper and wait for them to exit before I leave the bathroom stall.

I try to cool myself down before leaving the restroom by running my hands under the cold water. I am flushed, my face is red and there are beams of sweat on my forehead. Great! I look like I have the flu.

As I start to walk back to the table, I can see Darren and his parents in a tense discussion. It looks heated and I don't know if I should walk up or if I should wait it out. Before I have a chance to turn around his mother catches my eye and waves me over.

"Okay well let's have Tiffany clear this up then." His mother motions for me to sit down and I do as I instructed.

"I am sorry what do you need me to clear up for you?" I look confused and when I glance over at Darren, he looks horrified and mouths that he is sorry.

"Dear, I went to wash my hands and I heard you in the bathroom throwing up. Is there something you need to tell us?" She looks right at me. Doesn't blink or break a smile.

How can she know I am pregnant? Just by me throwing up. Darren did just tell her I am getting over a stomach bug. I take a big gulp of my water and decide to put on my big girl panties.

"Look, Darren and I never meant for this to happen, but we are both extremely excited and I hope you both will be happy for us too." I look over at Darren and he puts his face in his hands and starts to shake his head.

Okay now I am really confused. Wasn't that what she was implying since she heard me throwing up? That I am pregnant? What else could she have been referring to? Darren looks at both his parents and then back at me.

"Mom, Dad Tiffany is not bulimic." Darren grabs my hand

in his, "Tiffany, my mother thinks you were in the bathroom making yourself throw up. I told her you would never do that, but she insists that must be why you were throwing up because you barely touched your food and refused your mimosa."

I am shocked and I know I cannot control the horrific look on my face. I am so embarrassed that they think I would do that. I mean nothing against those that do, I know it's a disease and it is something not to take lightly, but they barely know me, and to jump to that conclusion over anything else is crazy.

Before I have a chance to fix what I almost blurted out, Darren's mother speaks up, "Wait. What do you mean you are both excited and we should be too?"

His mother looks panicked and grabs a hold of Mr. Hart's hand for support. They both look confused and freaked out at the same time.

I am upset and pissed and probably not thinking in the right frame of mind. I know I should have let Darren tell them, being he is their son, but if I am going to be involved with this family, I need to be able to show them I can hold my own.

"Mr. and Mrs. Hart. Darren and I wanted to wait a few more weeks before we told anyone, but last week we found out we are having a baby. I am sorry you are finding out this way. I would have loved for us to spend some more time together and we were able to share the news differently, but you didn't give me much of an option."

I look over at Darren and he nods his head that he is okay with what I said. Darren's parents are speechless. They don't respond. They just stare at us with blank looks on their face. After what feels like an hour, Darren's dad is the first one to speak up.

"Darren, how could you let this happen son? How can you be so careless to get someone you have been seeing for a few months pregnant? I thought we raised you smarter than this." His father is starting to look angry and his face is getting red.

Darren throws his napkin on the table and stands up. "Excuse me, careless? I understand this wasn't planned, but I assure you I am not being careless. I am in love with Tiffany, and yes, it might have happened earlier then we both wanted, but it would have happened eventually one day."

I stay seated not sure what I should do. I want to be respectful, and I still deep down want them to like me.

"Darren, you can't be serious. You barely know this girl." His mother rolls her eyes and takes a sip of her mimosa.

And that was it. That was the last straw. Darren calmly scoots his chair back, then helps me get out of my chair. Darren opens his wallet and grabs a couple of hundred dollar bills and tosses them on the table.

"I hope you enjoy the rest of your brunch. When you are ready to speak to me and Tiffany with respect and apologize, give me a call." Darren motions for me to leave by holding out his hand and I start to walk ahead of him toward the lobby.

I can hear Darren's father yelling, telling him to turn back around. I don't look back to see if he listened. I just keep walking toward the exit. I am so devastated not to mention humiliated. I knew something like this was going to happen. I can't believe how his parents reacted. First, they thought I was bulimic. Bulimic! And then they freak out that I am pregnant. Okay, I can understand not being on board with the pregnancy and I get this wasn't the way we wanted to tell them, but they didn't leave us any choice. I walk outside and wait for Darren to join me. He quickly walks through the door and walks directly toward the valet to hand them his ticket.

I feel so bad. I don't want to be the reason why Darren and his parents are not speaking. I walk toward Darren and hold his hand while we wait for the car.

"Darren, I am so sorry. I thought she found out I was pregnant. I had no idea she thought I had an eating disorder." I start to cry.

"Tiffany you did not do anything wrong, you hear me. It's my parents who did something wrong." He squeezes my hand to let me know he is not mad.

Darren lets my hand go and turns to me, placing his hand on my stomach. "If they cannot be happy for us and our baby, then screw them."

He leans in to kiss me as the car pulls up. He helps me get into the car and then tips the Valet as he gets in on the driver's side. He adjusts the seat because the Valet was a lot shorter than him and makes sure everything is in place, before putting the car in drive. As we are starting to pull away, we see his parents walk out of the hotel and stare at both of us. His father looks mad and his mother is crying. They don't speak to us or try and stop us from driving off. They just stand there and watch us leave.

Darren starts to drive away and I can hear him mumble under his breath that they need to pull the stick out of their ass. I am thankful that Darren stood up for me and our baby and I am thankful that he didn't stay there and argue, making me feel more uncomfortable than I already did. But I know he has a good relationship with his parents, and now they are not speaking because of me. I didn't want this to happen.

We both don't want to go home. Instead we go get ice cream and take a walk around the park. It's too nice outside to stay in, and right now I don't think I could be cooped up inside with my mind racing the way it is. Ice cream hits the spot. I get my favorite; chocolate fudge brownie and he chose vanilla with nuts and caramel. We walk around and eat our ice cream, neither of us really talking. I can tell he is a mile away from me.

"Darren, I know we have time, and it's still really early, but we should think about our living arrangements in the next few months. We will need a bigger place with the baby coming." I finish eating my ice cream and toss it in the trash can.

"Yea I was thinking about that too. I think we should look at buying a house together. Nothing too big, but maybe something close to here, on the water." Darren smiles and I can see his eyebrows go up, waiting for my response.

A house? He wants to buy a house. We are not even engaged or even talked about it. Besides I know I won't be able to afford anything he could. I guess Darren could tell what I was thinking because he starts laughing.

"Tiffany, please stop stressing. I want to support you and our baby. I can buy us a house and whatever else we need. If we are going to be a family, we need to stop thinking as mine and yours and start thinking of it as ours." Darren smiles and tries to kiss me with the caramel stuck to his lips. I laugh trying to push him away but he reaches my lips before I can stop him, smearing caramel on the side of my face. He has a way of making me feel better when I am down or stressing over something.

I don't know how I got so lucky. I love Darren Hart and I can't believe I am having his baby.

CHAPTER TWENTY

Today is the big day. It's Maggie and Ryan's wedding. Today is going to be a happy day. Nothing can ruin it for our family. I keep repeating that in my head over and over as I drive to the hotel where we are all getting ready. I have been practicing my fake smile and happy, positive attitude in the mirror, but it's been hard. Ever since the blow-up with Darren and his parents, he has been distant, working a lot and avoiding any talk about his parents whatsoever.

Yesterday was our first baby appointment. His attitude changed during the doctor's appointment and he seemed back to himself for the hour we were there. After we returned home, he saw a miss call from his father's office and his attitude went back to the way it was before, distant and short. I don't know what I should say or if it will make matters worse. On the positive side we did get an ultrasound. It was amazing seeing the little blip on the screen. It was still too early to hear the heartbeat but according to the size and my last period, the doctor thinks I am about 8 weeks pregnant. It's amazing how life works. Dr. Amelia said everything looks great and to just take it easy. She gave me some prenatal vitamins to start taking and said I am due back in 2 months unless I have any discomfort.

I pull into the Marina hotel and park my car. I take a few deep breaths before gathering enough strength to get out. I know soon as I enter my sister's hotel suite, it will be laughing, screaming, champagne toasts and more. I carefully remove my dress from the back seat and gather my purse and makeup bag before heading up to meet everyone else. I see my parents in the lobby welcoming the out of town guests who are arriving early and helping them check into their hotel rooms. My parents look so happy and proud. My father looks taller in a way and my mother is glowing. I hope I get to do this one day for my child. I rub my stomach. I still can't believe I am having a baby.

"Hey guys, I didn't think I would see you this early. How is Maggie, have you seen her yet?" I try to touch base with my parents before heading up. I know this day is going to be crazy.

"Yes, she is upstairs sweetheart, room 302. Where is Darren, I thought he would be with you?" My mom is so nosy sometimes, but I love her.

"No Darren had to work a little this morning and then he is heading over to be with Ryan until the wedding." I make it sound like it's normal and no big deal that he is working, but in all honesty he has been working a lot lately and I think everyone can sense something is going on between us. My mom gave me a weird look the other day when Darren didn't come over to have dinner with the rest of the family.

I tell my parent's good-bye and head up to see Maggie and help her get ready for her big day. Soon as I walk into her room, I hear music and the makeup artist has started doing her makeup.

"Well good morning my beautiful sister, and bride to be. How are we?" I give my sister a quick kiss on the cheek before listening to her rant about how the florist called and said they will be a little late.

I pull up a chair next to her and let her finish venting before changing the subject. We start reminiscing about when we were younger, we would play wedding in the backyard and that seems to work and put her in a better mood. For the next hour, we are laughing and singing and enjoying the time we have together. The makeup artist finally finishes and when Maggie turns around, I try to hold back tears. She is beautiful. Her makeup is subtle but her eyes pop. It's perfect for her. It's my turn to get my makeup done, but before I sit down, I pour us all a mimosa, mine just being orange juice but they don't need to know that.

I sit in the chair and show the lady an idea off my phone of how I want my makeup done. I have been looking through Pinterest all morning and finally found one I love. For the most part, it's cool tones but I want my eyes to stand out. She reassures me she knows exactly what I am talking about, and she starts her magic.

After 2 hours of getting our makeup and hair done, more champagne toasts, a few visits from our mom and Ryan's mom, we start to get dressed. The photographer will be here soon. I help Maggie get into her dress, and it is almost perfect when the song "Incomplete" starts playing by James Bay. Maggie looks at me through the reflection in the mirror. She smiles at me and I can see it in her face that she is truly happy and in love. She is ready for her big day, and I am so happy for her.

We arrive at the marina and after 30 minutes of taking pictures, it's time to head down to the room where we wait before Maggie is queued to walk down the aisle. I check my phone before turning it on silent. I still haven't heard from Darren and it's been hours. I sent him a few messages, but he hasn't responded. I am sure he is with Ryan. If he didn't show, I know Ryan would have said something by now.

"What's the matter Tiffany, you look worried?" Maggie snaps me out of my deep thought, and I feel horrible.

"What, oh nothing. I was just imagining my day with Darren. But today is your day Maggie. Let's get you married." The music starts, and it is my queue to start walking down the aisle.

Soon as the doors open, and I move forward I look at the front and immediately lock eyes with Darren. Thank God he is standing up there and he didn't flake or forget. I smile and continue to walk down the aisle until I reach the front. Darren looks at me and smiles. It melts my heart and I can't wait until we can talk and hold each other. We have only been apart for a few hours, but I feel like I need to feel his touch.

Darren mouths to me that he loves me, and I look beautiful. I blow him a quick kiss before the music changes and its Maggies turn for her big bridal entrance.

Maggie starts to walk down the aisle, and she looks amazing. My dad walking next to her looks so proud. He is glowing and I don't think the smile on his face can get any bigger. The wedding ceremony is short and lasts about 15 minutes. They wanted something quick and it was perfect. They didn't want to have any readings from the bible or have anyone sing. The ceremony was simple and it fit them both perfectly.

While all the guests mingle during the cocktail hour, the bridal party takes pictures and we all congratulate Maggie and Ryan and tell them how perfect the ceremony was. Even though the florist was a little late, they still finished setting up on time so honestly everything went off without any issues.

Darren walks over to me and doesn't say anything. He just holds my hand and looks down at me and smiles. He doesn't have to say anything though. That look alone was all I need to be reassured everything is okay between us. I ask the photographer to take a few pictures of Darren and me when he is finished. I wanted a few shots of just us. We really don't have any and I want to remember this day forever.

I see Maggie and Ryan whispering to each other across the room and they look happy and in their own little world. Just as it should be. I want that for me and Darren and hopefully one day we will both have what my sister and now brother in law both have.

The ceremony was amazing, but the reception was just as awesome. The food was on point, the music was perfect, and everyone got up and danced. You can tell everyone was enjoying themselves. My feet are starting to kill me from dancing so much, but I don't care. Anytime a slow song comes on, I pull Darren on the dance floor and he doesn't complain once. He just holds me and we both dance to the music. It feels good being held in his arms. He hasn't complained he is tired, or he wants to sit and have another drink. He smiles and lets me have what I want. And I will make sure he is properly thanked later tonight for being such a good sport about everything.

The night starts to end, and the DJ announces that it is time to see the bride and groom off. He plays one more song while they say goodbye and thank their guests for celebrating their day with them. After giving them some space with their friends and the rest of the family, Darren and I walk over and say our goodbyes, wishing them a happy honeymoon.

I stand there and observe my sister. I hope she remembers this day because right now she is probably the happiest I have ever seen her. They leave tomorrow morning for Hawaii and I know she cannot wait. She has been talking nonstop for the last month about this trip and all the excursions she signed them up to do. I hope Ryan knows what he is getting himself into.

* * *

The next morning, I wake up to the smell of coffee and bacon. My stomach is rumbling which reminds me I haven't eaten a thing since dinner last night at the wedding. I make a mental note to start eating healthier now that I am eating for two. I get out of bed and head to the kitchen where I spot Darren putting a plate of bacon on the table.

"Well good morning, you. What is all this?" I stand on my tiptoes to give him a quick kiss on the lips before stealing a piece of bacon.

"Good morning, Peaches. Just making my woman and baby some breakfast before I head to the office." Darren doesn't make eye contact with me and I know it's on purpose. I know he feels guilty he got to work today.

"The office? It's Sunday." Just like that my mood goes from perky to sad in a matter of seconds. I don't know why he's distancing himself and is diving into work like this. Why is it so hard for men to have open communication? He needs to talk to his parents so we can get past all this drama.

I sit down at the table, and Darren walks over with the rest of the food and joins me. "I will only be gone for a few hours and then we have the rest of the day to do whatever you want. I know I have been working a lot, but it comes with the territory. I am part owner, and with me and my dad not talking right now, it makes things difficult." Darren stops and looks at me to make sure I am okay.

Now I feel bad. I just learned he is the owner of a huge company, and I know I need to get on board with him working long hours and weekends. Being a writer, I am used to working when I want as long as I meet my deadline but being an owner you are never off the clock.

I make it a point to change my attitude so it's one less thing he needs to worry about. "I know, I am sorry. Of course, when you get home, maybe we can go shopping. I wouldn't mind looking at some baby stuff."

Darren's eyes light up and I know I hit the spot. "Yes, that sounds perfect, baby. I also started looking at houses this morning while I was waiting for you to wake up."

I stop buttering my toast is mid swipe and try to think carefully how I want to tell him I don't think that's a good idea. Us buying a house together.... That scares me.

"About that Darren. Maybe we should hold off for now. Buying a house together after only dating for 4 months. Don't you think that's moving too fast?" I hope he doesn't take this the wrong way.

"I don't see how that is faster than having a baby together. I mean we are already living together now. Why not do it with both of our names on the mortgage and a bigger place?" Darren looks at me and shrugs his shoulders after I don't respond.

He makes a valid point. And deep down I know he is right. I mean maybe I would feel better if we were engaged or something, but I am not bringing that up. I know we are far from that and we don't need anything else on our plate right now. We are still getting used to the idea of having a baby together, let alone plan a wedding.

"I know, you are right. Let's just not rush into it. Let's take our time, we can look, and if the right house comes along, then we can talk." I finish my breakfast and push my plate forward.

"Deal." Darren stands up and takes both of our plates to the kitchen to rinse them off.

"Here let me do that. The faster you leave and deal with work, the faster you can come home to me." I take the plate from his hand and start loading it into the dishwasher. Darren leaves and I finish wiping down the kitchen and table before I head back into our room and make the bed. I make a mental note to pick up some new sheets while we are out today.

After I finish getting ready, I grab the keys and head toward the door. I want to surprise Darren and make him a nice dinner tonight. I am thinking of steak and twice-baked potatoes with zucchini and squash. Healthy and delicious. I haven't been cooking that much lately with everything going on but now that the wedding planning and trips are over, I have more time to plan and cook meals. Even if I only make dinner a few times a week that's better than nothing.

I'm turning the handle to open the door and I hear a knock. I freeze, panicking slightly. The last time this happened it was Todd and that ended horribly for everyone. I peak through the hole in the door and take a step back. It is not Todd. Not even close. Standing right on the other side of the door is Mr. and Mrs. Hart. I take a deep breath and open the door. I have no idea why they are here, but I am about to find out.

"Mr. and Mrs. Hart, what are you doing here?" I try to be as polite as I can, but our last interaction together makes it extremely hard.

"Hi Tiffany, we wanted to talk to you and Darren before we leave for Georgia tonight. May we come in?" Mr. Hart points to my apartment and for a quick moment I forgot where I was.

"Yes of course, please come in. But Darren isn't here. He had to run to the office for a few hours." I step aside and motion for them to come in.

Mrs. Hart takes a seat on the couch in the living room and Mr. Hart follows, sitting next to her.

"I am afraid we started off on the wrong foot. We never meant to offend you, or Darren and I hope you will forgive us. I was just surprised that's all. I am sure you understand we are just very protective of Darren." Mrs. Hart sounds sincere but lately I feel like I have a horrible judge of character. I also thought she was sweet before she accused me of having an eating disorder.

"Well thank you for apologizing. I hope you know I would never do anything to hurt Darren or jeopardize him or his career in any way. I don't want his money and up until a few weeks ago, I had no idea he is part owner of H & H solutions." I try to be as honest as I can without sounding like I am trying to persuade them.

"We know dear. That is why we are here. We want to be involved in Darren's life along with yours and the baby. Therefore, we want to make amends." Darren's father stands up and walks toward the window.

"We want you and Darren to move to Georgia, where he can run the company from our main office." Mr. Hart turns around and I can tell he is dead serious.

He wants us to move to Georgia. Why? I don't understand, but I have a feeling there is something else going on that they haven't mentioned yet.

"Yes dear, you both move to Georgia. You guys can live in one of our homes where you can raise the baby. We can supply a nanny to help you. You are just a writer so I am sure you can do that from anywhere." Mrs. Hart waves her hand like she is dismissing me.

Just a writer. Where does she get off downplaying my career? I am a bad as writer and journalist and I have no problem supporting myself and my baby without Darren or their help.

"Of course, when the time is right and should you and Darren choose to get married, you will need to sign a prenup. But like you said you are not after his money, so I am sure you won't care." Mr. Hart walks back over to where I am sitting and looks at his watch.

"What the hell are you both doing here?" Darren is standing in the doorway with the door open, looking angry as hell.

I jump not expecting to hear Darren's voice and I know that letting them both in was probably a huge mistake on my part, but I couldn't be rude to his parents if we want to try and work this out.

Mrs. Hart stands up looking frantic, "Darren we only want what is best for you."

"What's best? Telling my girlfriend her job doesn't matter, and telling her she needs to sign a prenup is what's best for me? You both need to understand something. I love Tiffany. She will not be signing anything. And if you do not accept her wholeheartedly then you do not accept me. Do you understand?" Darren lets the front door slam closed and starts walking toward the living room.

"Darren don't speak to us like that. We came to apologize and try and make amends. We like Tiffany and want to get to know her better. I would ask anyone to sign a prenup. It has nothing to do with her specifically." Darren's father holds his hand out and Mrs. Hart takes it. They start to walk toward the door and Darren moves to open it for them.

"I need to talk to Tiffany. I will call you later. Next time, please call me before stopping by so I make sure I am available for these little chats." Darren closes the door after his parents leave and he leans his forehead on the back of the door.

I don't know what to say. I know I probably shouldn't have let them in, but I thought they just wanted to make amends and not throw out an ultimatum.

"Darren, please I was on my way out when they showed up. I didn't want to be rude to your parents so I....." Darren holds his hand up and I stop talking.

He turns around, shaking his head, "You don't need to apologize. I am not mad at you. You did nothing wrong and I should be the one apologizing for how my parents are treating you."

I don't know if it's my emotions or I am just exhausted, but I start crying. I don't know what I can do to prove to his parents that I am not some gold digger except to sign the prenup.

"Darren, if and when we decide to get married, and please don't take this like I am expecting a proposal anytime soon, I am fine with signing a prenup if that proves to your parents I am not after your money." I wipe my eyes and try to calm myself down, but the tears just keep coming.

Darren kneels in front of me so he can look at me. "Baby listen to me. The reason I will never allow you to sign a prenup is that I know you are not after my money. I also want to make sure you and our family is taken care of should anything ever happen to me. Signing a prenup is out of the question."

Darren wipes the tears from my eyes. "The reason why I left this morning was not to go to work. It was to speak to your father."

My heads shot up so fast, I almost pulled a muscle. "Why?" Why in the world would he tell me he is going to work when he went to see my father?

"Tiffany I was going to wait and surprise you with a weekend trip to do this, but I don't think I can." Darren pulls a blue box out of his pocket and opens the top. Sitting there is a beautiful diamond ring.

I start crying and shaking my head in disbelief. Is he for real? I can't believe this is happening right now.

"Tiffany you are the love of my life and the mother to our future baby. I couldn't imagine spending my life without you. Please will you say yes, and be my wife?" Darren holds open the box and the ring is glistening at me.

I can't imagine living my life without Darren. Meeting each other in the middle of nowhere, in a dive bar and then running into each other again at my parents' house must be fate. I have always believed that things happen for a reason, so I know that Darren and I were meant to meet and be together. I want to marry Darren, but things are moving way to fast, and I feel like I have no control.

I start crying and shake my head yes. "Darren, I love you, and I want to marry you someday, but I think we should wait. Everything seems to be moving so fast and out of my control. It's all too overwhelming."

He slides the ring on my finger and leans forward giving me a hug. His head is cradled in my neck and I can feel him take a deep breath.

"Tiffany, I am not asking you to marry me tomorrow. We can have a long engagement. But I want to marry you and be a family. I want you to know that you and our baby mean the world to me." He looks up and I can tell he is for real. I have never felt surer of anyone before in my life.

"Okay Darren Hart. I will marry you and be your wife. But let's take it slow and enjoy our engagement. We don't need to rush." I hug Darren and look at the ring on my hand. It's beautiful and I couldn't have picked out a prettier ring myself.

It's a platinum ring with small diamonds in the band that wraps around, and a solitaire princess cut diamond in the middle.

It's beautiful and I couldn't have imagined him proposing with any other ring.

* * *

I can't believe I have to wait a week to tell Maggie and Ryan we are engaged and pregnant. Her head is going to explode with the news. If anyone would have guessed a year ago this is where I would be right now, I would have called them crazy. The last 8 months have been both amazing and rocky to say the least. I thought my world was ending 8 months ago when I found my ex-finance cheating on me with my best friend. All at once I lost my job, future husband and best friend, but the reality was it wasn't ending, it was just beginning. I just didn't know it at the time.

Now the real question is will Darren's family finally accept us being together as a couple and as part of the family or will they continue to cause problems. One thing I know for sure is I won't let anyone treat my child with disrespect... I don't care how much money they have or who they are.

Thank you for reading the 1ˢᵗ book in the
Falling for Hart Series.
Please subscribe to my author page for exciting
announcements on my upcoming books.
Facebook: @Words by Renee

Made in the USA
Columbia, SC
17 May 2020